Offside

AND
OFF-LIMITS

KATE O'KEEFFE

Map of the Town

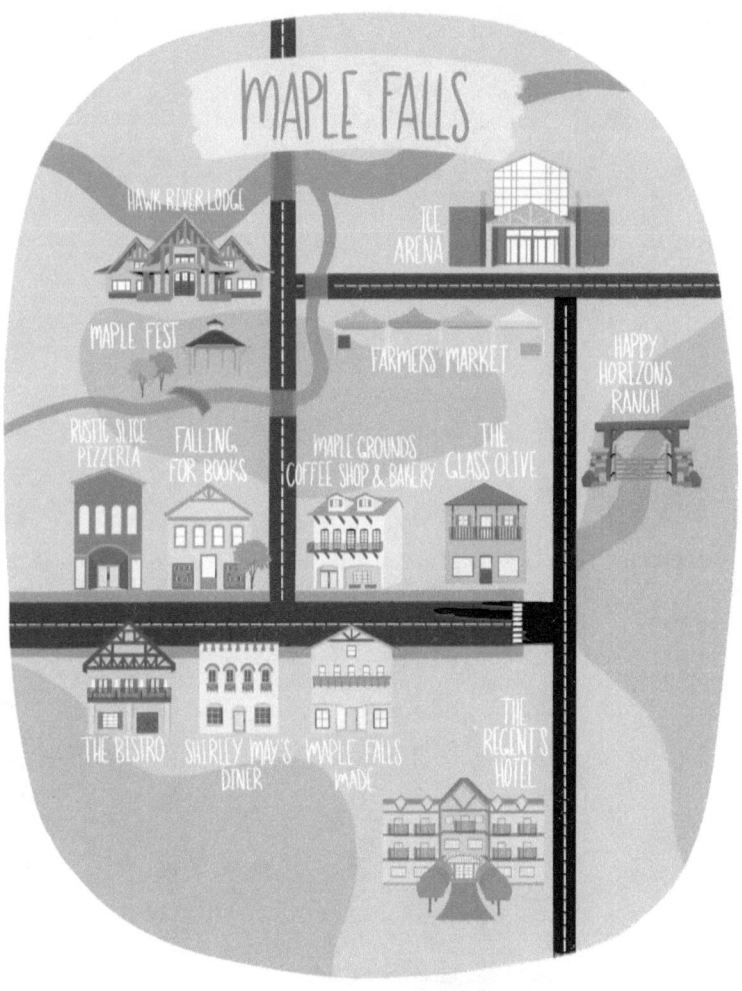

CHAPTER 1
CLARA

BALANCING a paper bag of groceries on each hip, I slide the key into the front door lock and push the door open with my hip. I'm doing my best to listen to my daughter tell me all about her school day—and I do mean *all* about it, thanks to the fact she inherited my lack of conciseness—as my son uses my butt as his own personal drum machine.

Motherhood. Am I right?

"—which is why I told Mrs. Englewood that you would bake *all* the cupcakes and that you would do the fancy thing with the sprinkles that you know me and my friends love so much, right, Mommy?" Hannah says, at long last taking a breath.

"You did what?" I ask as I trudge down the hallway and into the kitchen. "Close the door behind you, please, Benny!"

The house rattles as he slams the door shut.

"I said *close* the door, Benny, not cause roof tiles to drop off."

He doesn't reply.

"He always does that," Hannah says, her arms crossed, relishing it as she always does when Benny gets told off.

I place the heavy grocery bags on the kitchen counter and let out a relieved sigh. Being a single mom should come with a warning label. *Do not take if allergic to noise, repetition, or having to negotiate peace talks between people under the height of five foot nothing.*

"So you'll do it, Mommy?" Hannah asks.

I turn to look at her and see that hopeful smile on her pretty, young face. Her hair is still in the braids I did over cornflakes this morning, the same blonde as both mine and her aunt Keira's. "How many cupcakes exactly, sweetheart?"

"It's for the bake sale so lots and lots and lots."

"So, like, twenty?" I ask hopefully as I mentally calculate how long it will take me to bake twenty cupcakes, allow them to cool, and then ice them all. Perfectly doable before leaving the house for school tomorrow morning.

"Oh, more than that. I told Mrs. Englewood a hundred."

I widen my eyes. "A hundred? Sweetheart, there's no way I can make that many in one evening when we've got to take Benny to hockey practice and you've got figure skating class. It's not humanly possible."

"Please, Mommy?" she asks, doing that pleading thing she's perfected over the years that I'm almost certain she got while watching Puss in Boots in the *Shrek* movies. Her blue eyes are the size of saucers.

"I'll do what I can," I tell her, wishing I could magic up one hundred perfectly frosted cupcakes with a snap of my fingers— and knowing I'll be elbow deep in cake mix until after midnight.

"Thanks, Mommy," she says with a smile that lights up her

entire face, bouncing on the spot as though she has too much energy to contain inside her little body.

Which is about exactly the opposite of me.

Benny charges into the room, wielding his hockey stick as though it's a sword. He comes to a sudden stop when his stick meets the wall, puncturing a hole in the plaster. "Oops," he says, looking up at me with a grimace.

Hannah crosses her arms and glares at her brother. "You broke the kitchen wall, Benny. You are in so much trouble."

"I didn't mean it!" Benny says, his voice a high-pitched whine the neighborhood dogs are probably pricking their ears up at.

I blow out a frustrated breath as I inspect the damage. "How many times do I have to tell you not to run around with your hockey stick inside, Benny?"

"Too many times," mini-me replies.

"I didn't mean it," is his repeated reply, like somehow that means the wall won't be punctured and I won't have to either hide it up with one of the kids' drawings or go to the expense of getting it fixed.

The drawing, it is.

My phone rings as I'm running my fingers over the dent in the wall.

"Mommy, your phone is ringing," Benny tells me, thrusting my phone in front of my face, almost hitting my nose.

I take it and read the screen. Instantly, my heart begins to drum in my chest. I straighten up and hold my index finger up against my lips to tell the kids to be quiet.

This is it. My shot.

I straighten my shoulders and press answer, putting on my best phone voice. "Hello, Clara Johnson speaking," I say, even though the caller ID has told me exactly who it is on the other end.

"Clara, hi. It's Veronica Reynolds from the Ice Breakers management team."

"Hello, Ms. Reynolds," I reply, keeping my voice as steady as I can manage. Which is no small feat when you've got one child's set of eyes trained on you, while the other child is reaching for his hockey stick once more, ready to inflict more damage on our home.

"You're going to be sent to your room for the rest of the day for breaking the wall," Hannah says as she makes a grab for his hockey stick.

"I am not!" Benny rebuffs, yanking on the stick.

"Yes, you are!" Hannah replies.

I place my hand on the offending weapon and glare at both my offspring as I say, "Bear with me a moment, please, Ms. Reynolds."

"Of course," she replies, and I wonder how much of Benny's exchange she heard.

Placing my hand over the speaker, I say, "I'll have the stick, thank you. Now both of you, go get changed, ready to go to your lessons."

To my utter astonishment both kids do as I say, leaving me alone in the kitchen, holding the hockey stick in one hand and my phone in the other.

Miracles like this are few and far between in parenting.

"Sorry about that," I say to Veronica Reynolds.

"It sounds like you've got your hands full, Clara."

"Not at all," I reassure her because what does *that* mean? You're too busy to take the job? You're better off remaining a stay-at-home mom who works part-time doing a mind-numbing admin job for a local accounting firm?

"I'm calling with good news, Clara. You really impressed us in your interview. We would love to offer you the job of Social Media Manager for the Ice Breakers."

Suddenly holes in the wall and arguing kids melt into the background.

"Are you serious?" My voice veers more toward the squeaky mouse end of the scale than the, *I'm totally in control and get awesome job offers every day of the week* that I'm aiming for. In my defense, this is my absolute dream job, and I'd already convinced myself I didn't get it to lessen the blow when I got the news.

She laughs. "Of course I'm serious. We loved your social media ideas. They were so fresh and fun."

Wow. Not only am I getting offered the job, but I'm getting complimented by Veronica Reynolds, Chief Marketing Officer for the Ice Breakers, and altogether impressive businesswoman. Aka, who I would love to be, given half the chance.

"Thank you so much. That means a lot coming from you," I gush.

"Flattery will get you everywhere, Clara." I can hear the smile in her voice.

"I'll remember that," I reply, my giddiness threatening to roll out of me in an excited squeak. But I'm aiming for non-mouse here, so I do my best to hold it in.

"Not only did you impress in the interview, but the strong, authentic voice in your existing social media presence showed us your authentic self in an interesting way. We think you'll be a real asset to the Ice Breakers."

It had felt like a risk at the time to use my @CFSMomLife as a reference point for what I'm capable of online. I started the account soon after my diagnosis with chronic fatigue many years ago, and the online community that I hooked into has grown to be such an important part of my wellness journey.

And the fact I've got a decent following these days can't have hurt, either.

"So my CFS isn't an issue?" I ask and hold my breath.

"We're an equal opportunities employer at the Ice Breakers, Clara. We only employ the best, regardless of their personal circumstances, and you have successfully used social media to share your story and inspire others. In a crowded online world where it's hard to get heard, that's quite an achievement. Unless, of course, you're posting funny cat videos."

I let out a relieved laugh. "I don't even own a cat."

Even though I've been doing great for well over a year now, I still felt it was super important to be upfront with Veronica about my CFS. Experience has shown me that even though I have many "green light days," as my friend, doctor, and Chronic Warriors Support Group leader, Bernice Chen, puts it, I don't have endless energy reserves. I need to manage myself carefully —which means sleep, nutrition, exercise, and me time.

Some of this is a big ask for a single mom who's taken whatever jobs she could, just to keep the lights on.

And in recovery from CFS, you never know when your symptoms can come back and bite you on the butt.

"It was a unanimous decision to bring you on board. When Kaylee left so suddenly during this crucial pre-season, quite honestly, we wondered how we could ever replace her. But you, Clara Johnson, you impressed us all with your fresh approach and enthusiasm for the role."

"I appreciate that so much. Thank you."

"So? What do you say? Will you be the Ice Breakers' new social media manager, aka SMM?" she asks, and then adds, "We do so love an acronym."

"Of course I will! Are you kidding? Thank you so, so much, Ms. Reynolds," I then reply in a rush.

"Veronica, please. Everyone in the office is on a first name basis."

"Got it," I echo.

"When can you start? With the players already in pre-season training, it would be great to get you on board soon. You could start by getting some footage of their training sessions. Our followers love to see our players doing their thing on the ice."

"How does Monday sound?" I ask, my stomach full of excited butterflies. That will give me enough time to hand in my notice to the accountants and mentally prepare for this new challenge.

And it's going to be a challenge for me. Becoming the Ice

Breakers' Social Media Manager will be my first ever serious job. And yes, I know that sounds terrible for a 31-year-old woman to admit.

The thing is, I got married and quickly pregnant with Hannah so early in my time at college that I never actually graduated. Instead, I moved back home to Maple Falls with my ex, Dwayne, to live in my childhood home that my parents had left to me and my sister Keira when they'd passed away in a car crash years before. Dwayne went out to work, and I became a stay-at-home mom.

Then Benny came along, and it seemed my fate was set. A husband, two kids, and bills to pay meant I would take whatever work I could get, working part time as a waitress at Shirley May's diner, handing out skate rentals at the arena, serving coffee at Falling for Books, Emmy Roberts's place on Main Street.

You name a business in this small town, and you can bet your bottom dollar I've worked there.

It wasn't what I had dreamed of, but you know what? I wouldn't change it. Although things didn't work out with Dwayne, I got my two beautiful babies, Hannah and Benny.

Together, they are the light of my life.

And life was good for a while. Well, for a few years at least. One winter, I caught a particularly nasty virus when the kids were still in preschool, a virus I never quite got over, finally getting diagnosed with CFS.

And then my whole world imploded.

That's why this job means so much to me.

"Monday is perfect, Clara. I'll have the contract sent over to you this afternoon, and we can get together first thing Monday morning and talk about putting some of your great ideas into practice."

My great ideas. No pressure.

"That sounds wonderful, Ms.—I mean Veronica."

"You'll get used to it. See you Monday, eight thirty."

"I look forward to it," I reply, and she clicks off with a cheery goodbye.

I let out a breath.

I got the job. I got the job!

I'm the new Social Media Manager for the Ice Breakers.

Me, Clara Johnson, college dropout, single mom, and CFS survivor.

No more filing, data entry, or answering phones for Mr. Walker and his team of cardigan-wearing accountants. Nope. I'm going to be devising and executing social media campaigns for the biggest, most exciting team in the history of Maple Falls, full to the brim of new players, ready to take on the League and prove their worth.

And I'm only *half* scared to death.

CHAPTER 2
CADE

I MAKE my way across the hardwood floor of my new living room and come to a stop by the floor to ceiling windows overlooking the landscape.

And there's a *lot* of landscape in this new small town I'm calling home for the coming season. Which, if I'm honest, for a city guy like me, is a little unnerving.

Okay, it's a lot unnerving.

I'm used to traffic and bars and people everywhere, living in the heart of Manhattan where I can get a pizza delivered to my place on the forty-seventh floor at 3:00 a.m. and never worry about running into the same person twice.

Here in Maple Falls, trees outnumber the residents by about 5,000 to one.

I blow out a breath, staring out at some of those trees. It's mid-September and they're just beginning to turn, creating a palette of greens and reds and oranges. The sun is high in the sky, partly obscured by clouds, with darkness on the horizon.

Here comes that famous Washington state rain.

I've been in Maple Falls for less than twenty-four hours, and although it's the complete opposite of the frenetic buzz of where I used to live, the place sure does have a certain small-town charm to it, much like those Hallmark Christmas movies my mom loves to watch.

I spent my first night at a lodge, breakfasting at a quaint diner on Main Street, run by a woman who came out to introduce herself as Shirley May, her eyes twinkling as she accurately guessed I was one of the new hockey players in town.

I meandered down Main Street, checking out the old-fashioned buildings and feeling like I'd not only just flown from the other side of the country, but that I'd stepped back in time like Marty McFly—only without a DeLorean and a pair of low-top Nikes.

After my hearty breakfast of eggs, bacon, and a stack of pancakes, I walked back to my black BMW SUV, and it seemed every eye on Main Street was trained on me. A couple of women threw me flirty smiles, and a boy of about eleven asked for a selfie with me. Of course I obliged. This is the kind of place where everyone is up in everyone else's business. As my new home for at least this season, I want to fit in.

"Where do you want this?" a gruff voice says, pulling my attention from all those trees, and I turn to see five workers manhandling my prized baby grand piano. Sweat is pouring from their brows, and I'm thankful my prized Bösendorfer is all wrapped up nice in protective blankets and cardboard.

I'm kinda precious about my Bess.

And yeah, I did give her a name. Me and Bess are the longest relationship I've ever had.

After paying off my mom's mortgage and putting a deposit on my own Manhattan place, Bess was the next thing I bought, thanks to the injection of cash signing with the NYC Blades brought.

We've been through a lot together. I couldn't leave her behind in the city, not even for this one season with the Ice Breakers.

"Over there in the corner, thanks, guys," I instruct them, pointing at an alcove by the fireplace. "Let me help."

"It's our job," Ralph, the team leader says, but I join the guys anyway, the familiar stench of sweat hitting my nostrils as we position Bess just so.

"You play this thing?" Ralph pulls a cloth handkerchief from his overalls pocket and begins to mop his brow as the members of his crew begin to remove the cardboard outer layer.

"Sure do. My mom got me lessons when I was a kid. She figured it was good for me to have interests outside of hockey," I reply, and a couple of the guys snicker, sharing knowing looks.

"Not including that," I add with an internal groan, knowing exactly what they're laughing at.

My reputation as a bad boy ladies' man has clearly followed me over to the West Coast.

But the thing is, I'm not that guy anymore. In fact, I haven't been that guy for well over a year now. Not that the media or even my teammates seem to have cottoned on to the fact yet. They still see me as the party guy, turning up with a woman on each arm and going home with another.

Don't get me wrong, that lifestyle was fun. *More* than fun. What young guy, fresh out in the world after college, doesn't want beautiful and available women throwing themselves at him 24/7? And all just because he's good at playing hockey.

It's a giant ego boost, and one I was happy to entertain.

There were lots of girls, but over time, I worked out that they didn't want to be with me, the poor kid from New Jersey who grew up with a single mom who had to work double shifts at a diner and made tote bags to sell at weekend markets, just to make ends meet.

They didn't want to know *that* guy.

They wanted the rich, fun-loving, partying winger for the New York City Blades, the guy who would happily splash the cash, get them into club VIP sections, buy bottles of Cristal, and get recognized in the street.

I playacted that guy for years. Heck, I *became* that guy.

But it wasn't real, and a part of me always knew it wouldn't last. You can't play pro hockey your whole life. Not even Marc-Andre Fleury could do that.

Then I hit my thirties and a bunch of my teammates began to settle down, some even starting families. Suddenly, the bachelor lifestyle lost its luster. It got old, all those parties, all those meaningless hook-ups. I wanted what those guys had, the ones who had met the one, who'd fallen in love, who'd committed themselves to one person for the rest of their lives.

There was this one guy on the Blades. Jethro Drake. He'd been one of my partners in partying crime, always up for going out on the town, always attracting a bevy of beauties wherever he went. And then he met Bella, a schoolteacher of all things, and it was like he had a total personality change overnight. One day he was party boy extraordinaire, and then the next he was accompanying Bella to her classroom after hours to decorate it with her students' artwork.

At first, I didn't get it. What was so special about this girl? But then I saw the way they looked at each other, and I felt it, right in my chest.

They were in love, and that wasn't an emotion I was all that familiar with.

Or at all.

It was then that I lost the taste for the party scene, the puck bunnies, all of it.

I wanted what Drake and Bella had. Only I had no clue how to go about getting it.

I still don't.

But that doesn't stop me from wanting it.

Of course I didn't tell anybody about my change of heart, and my reputation has clung to me like a baby koala clings to its mom.

That was close to two years ago, and I swear, time moves faster than it once did back in the good old days. Blink and it's two years later.

Man, getting old sucks.

But age does come with perks, including the fact that, as an Unrestricted Free Agent, I could intentionally sign with a team located not only across the country from where I'd played most of my professional life, but in a small town where I could get the chance to reinvent myself as the man I am now. Not the man I once was.

With Bess sitting in pride of place, I pull a Stanley knife from my back pocket and cut open a box. I pull out a framed photo of me, my mom, and my sister Tori and her two kids, taken last Thanksgiving. All of us are grinning at the camera. We'd just eaten our turkey dinner with Tori's husband, Lionel, my aunt Liz and uncle Don, and then played charades, the football game on the TV muted as we laughed at our terrible miming.

I wonder what this Thanksgiving will be like, now that I'm across the country from them all, playing on a new team, no longer able to drive over to New Jersey to see them.

When I told my mom I would move her to Maple Falls if it worked out for me here, she smiled like it was Christmas day. But there's no point in uprooting her life if this isn't going to be my forever home.

And I won't know that until I've settled in and found my feet.

"Nice place you got here, Lennox," a voice says, and I look up to see Jamie Hayes, my former NYC Blades captain and now fellow Ice Breaker, climbing over a bunch of boxes as he makes his way toward me.

"Hayes! Good to see you, my man," I say as I clasp his hand in mine and slap him on his back. Like me, he's in jeans and a hoodie.

"Good to see you, too, Lennox."

"I'd offer you a coffee, but I've got no clue how to use the fancy machine that came with this place." I gesture at the behemoth copper machine on one of the kitchen counters, looking like something from a Victorian locomotive.

"How's the unpacking going?"

"We're getting there," I say.

He looks down at one of the boxes by his feet, labeled "Comics." "You brought your comic books?"

"Of course I did," I reply as though he's asked me if I plan on breathing oxygen here in Maple Falls. "I've moved here, man. They go where I go. Period."

"Is that why you're always wearing tops with weird sayings?" He gestures at my black T-shirt with the words "Nexus Point" emblazoned across my chest.

"Don't play dumb with me. You know *The Timekeepers Chronicles* is da bomb."

He arches an eyebrow. "Da bomb?"

I chuckle. "You should get into them, man. There are so many twists and turns, plus the time travel warps your mind."

He chortles, shaking his head. "You do you, Lennox. I'm hoping you brought your gym equipment. This place is big enough for it all."

"Sure did. It's all set up in the garage, ready for use as and when. Wanna see?"

"Lead the way."

We make our way through the boxes and down the hallway, where I give Jamie a mini tour of the house before entering the garage. The equipment has all been unboxed, and I've spent the best part of a couple hours helping some of the guys put the machines together after my breakfast, courtesy of Shirley May.

Jamie casts an appreciative eye around the space. "It'll be just like NYC, us working out together."

"Mostly, yeah."

He arches an eyebrow at me. "Mostly?"

I chew on my lip for a beat. "I'm, well, I'm hoping this place will mean a fresh start for me."

"Are you thinking of getting another weights system?"

"Nah, I mean more along the lines of reinventing myself. Leaving the old Cade Lennox behind."

"New town, new you? Like a new hairdo if you're a chick?" he asks with a grin, and I laugh.

"Something like that, only less to do with hairstyles and more to do with how I choose to live my life."

He narrows his eyes at me. "Meaning?"

"You know me. I'm a good time guy. I love to party. I love to meet women. I don't do serious, and I don't do commitment."

"'Loverboy Lennox,' wasn't that one of the nicknames the media gave you a while back?"

I cringe. "Yeah."

"And 'Manhattan's Most Wanted.' I remember that one 'cos a bunch of the guys on the team were jealous. They wanted that one."

"They can have it. I'm done with all that."

"You're done with that whole rapper lifestyle you had going on?"

"Heck, yeah. I want—" I break off, thinking of the conversation I had with my mom last Thanksgiving. She told me she wanted me to have the world, and part of that was finding someone to share it with. I swallow. "I guess I want to make my mom proud of who I am as a man."

"Huh."

"What does *that* mean?"

He pats me on the back. "It means my boy is finally growing up."

I push his shoulder with the heel of my hand. "Shut up, man. I'm being serious here. I want to leave that guy behind. I want something more. Something real. Like Drake has with his girl."

"Drake fell hard, and fast."

"Yup."

"And you're expecting to meet the love of your life here in this small town? You do know the population is like a hundred people."

"More like ten thousand, isn't it?"

"You get what I mean. There are way fewer women in a small town than in a big place like the City."

I shrug. "Sure there are. It's basic math, Hayes."

He slaps me on the back once more. "Good luck with that."

"Thanks?"

He laughs. "I'm serious. If you want to change your life, Lennox, knock yourself out. Most of us want to leave bits of our past behind. I know I do, and turning over a new leaf in a place named after maple trees?"

"It's kinda poetic."

"As poetic as we hockey players get."

Later that evening, with the boxes now mostly unpacked, I sit at Bess, my fingers resting on her keys. I look over at the view through the living room windows. The sun is beginning to set, casting a warm glow over the trees, the sky streaked with clouds dipped in vibrant colors. I play a few notes and smile to myself.

This is where it's going to happen. This is my fresh start. This place is where I become the man I always knew I could be.

CHAPTER 3
CLARA

"BRING IT IN, Ms. Amazing Social Media Expert." My childhood friend, who has recently returned to Maple Falls, has her arms held out wide as she beams at me while standing outside Falling for Books on Main Street. The store is run by my sister's sister-in-law, Emmy, because this is Maple Falls, where everyone has fewer than two degrees of separation in our limited gene pool.

I step into Bailey's arms, and she squeezes me tight. "Thanks. But I'm just the social media manager, not exactly an expert."

She pulls back and smiles at me, her hands on my shoulders.

"You'll be an expert in no time, and you'll get promoted to Goddess of All Things before the year is out. I just know it."

I let out a laugh. "I'm not sure Goddess of All Things is an actual job title, at least not at the Ice Breakers."

She gives me another squeeze. "Isn't it just so great that we're both working for the League these days?"

"You're seasoned at this, having been bounced around the country on different teams. Me? Total novice."

As usual, my friend looks totally polished in a pair of jeans and a pale blue jacket, her blonde hair falling in soft waves around her shoulders, the smattering of freckles across her nose just the same as they were back in high school.

"Hey there," Bailey says, leaning down to my son's height. "You're Benny, right?" she asks and he nods. "I haven't see you since last Christmas. I think you've grown three feet since then."

Benny beams with pride, despite the fact he's probably grown only three inches in the past nine months.

I gesture at the entrance. "Shall we head in? Benny wants a comic book to celebrate me getting my new job."

"What a wonderful mom you have," Bailey says.

"She's okay," Benny replies before bounding into the store.

Bailey quirks an eyebrow. "High praise indeed."

"That's mom life for you," I reply on a sigh.

We step inside the store and immediately, I'm hit by the smell of coffee and sweet baked goods wafting in the air from the coffee shop at the back of the store.

"Coffee? My treat to celebrate your new job," Bailey offers as we follow Benny through the books to the comic section. "Or would you prefer a comic book?"

I laugh. "Coffee would be great. Thanks, Bailey."

We reach the counter where we're greeted by Maple Falls' queen of cupcakes, Neesha, along with Emmy, aka Keira's sister-in-law and the owner of Falling for Books.

Limited gene pool, remember?

"Hey, Clara. Mrs. McCluskey told me about the new job. That's awesome!" Emmy says with a broad smile.

"Yeah, congratulations," Neesha says.

"Thanks a lot," I reply, not in the least surprised to learn that they've already heard about my new position. Even the tiniest piece of news travels faster than a road runner on an exercise kick in this town, particularly if Mary-Ellen McCluskey is involved.

"By the sounds of things, you're going to be getting up close and personal with all those hunky hockey players," Emmy says with a waggle of her eyebrows.

I laugh. Emmy and Dawson Hayes have been together for ages. Dawson was one of the first batch of Ice Breakers to hit town, the ones who played for charity. And just like my sister, Keira, she's ridiculously happy and loved-up these days.

It's nice for some.

"Emmy, remind me. Aren't you engaged to a hunky hockey player?" I tease.

"Sure am," Emmy replies, her eyes soft. "You know there's a new bunch of guys in town now that the Ice Breakers are part of the League. You could snag one of them for yourself. That's what I told Neesha."

Neesha rolls her eyes. "She did. Not that I listened. I'm not interested in hockey players"

"Good for you," I say to her.

Being practically the only single female residents left in this town under the age of thirty-five, I'm positive both Neesha and I are going to be matched up with the new guys in town, whether we like it or not.

"Never say never, Clara," Emmy says.

"I say never, and so does the non-fraternization clause in my new employment contract," I reply.

Emmy's features drop. "Seriously?"

"That's too bad," Bailey adds.

I scrunch up my nose. "Is it?"

"I don't know. It might just be that I have a certain bias toward hockey players," Emmy replies.

"Enough hockey talk. What can I get you two ladies?" Neesha asks.

"What flavor cupcakes do you have today?" I ask.

"Cookies and cream, raspberry and white chocolate, maple and walnut, and a new recipe I'm trying out: key lime," Neesha replies proudly.

"Key lime," both Bailey and I say in unison. "And two lattes, please," I add.

I glance over to see Benny riffling through the small comic book collection Emmy has at the bookstore, searching for whatever title he decides I need to buy him next. He's already amassed quite the collection, and his current obsession is with a series called *The Timekeeper Chronicles*. I don't get it, but he loves it, and that's what matters.

Bailey and I take a seat at one of the small tables within eyesight of him, hanging our jackets over the backs of the wooden chairs.

"So, tell me everything about this new job of yours."

"Well, I'll be responsible for all the social media activity for the team, starting with creating a content schedule so I can plan what to post, and when and where to post it. Then I'll create the content to post. I'll be monitoring analytics from them as well as staying updated on social media trends and platform changes. I'll need to collaborate with graphic designers for visual assets, responding...to...fans..." I trail off when I notice Bailey's eyebrows are raised. "What?"

"I just want to know the fun part."

"What do you mean? That *is* the fun part."

"No, I mean things like getting the players to do TikTok dances or trick shot challenges. That kind of thing."

"Trick shot challenges?" I ask as I pull my phone from my purse and add it to my list entitled *Ice Breaker Engagement Ideas*. "I like that."

"Not the TikTok dances? Those would be a lot of fun. Those big, sporty guys doing all those dance moves is a real crowd pleaser. The social media manager did a bunch with the teams I've worked with before."

"Maybe?" I say elusively as I place my phone down on the table.

"What does that mean?"

I shrug. "It's been done before."

"Because they can be so good! Look at these." It's Bailey's turn to get out her phone, and she pulls up a bunch of videos of hockey players dancing to different degrees of synchronized success. "See? You've got to do some with the team. People will go crazy for them."

Neesha delivers our coffee and cupcakes, and we thank her. "Let me know what you think of the key lime flavor," she says.

"We will," Bailey and I chant, and she makes her way back to the counter where Mary-Ellen McCluskey is waiting.

I shoot her a quick wave before I return my attention to my friend.

"Do you really have a non-fraternization clause in your employment contract?" Bailey asks as she takes a sip of her coffee.

"Sure do. And besides, after the drama that is my ex, I've got zero interest in meeting some new guy."

"Even if he's a hot hockey player?"

"*Especially* if he's a hot hockey player," I say with a laugh. "They're not exactly known to be one-woman men."

"There are a couple players from the New York City Blades in this year's team, including the Ice Breakers' new captain."

"Jamie Hayes. I've been studying up. I've got a spreadsheet with stats on all the guys, including photos of them all so I know who they are when I meet them Monday, as well as the sorts of things they've done on social media before. One of the guys on the team got pranked in one of those 'snake in the cooler' things last season. The video went viral."

"Is that when someone places a fake snake in a cooler and someone videos the player's reaction when they open it up to get a drink?" she asks, and I nod. "You've got to admit that sounds a lot more fun than spreadsheets and monitoring analytics."

I shrug as I lift my coffee to my lips and take a sip. "It's all part of the job."

"What does Mystery Man think?"

I mentioned the guy I've been chatting with online for the last few months to Bailey when we were messaging once, and she asks after him every time, always calling him Mystery Man, even though I've pointed out more than once his name is Warrior.

Well, not his real name. I don't know who he is exactly because we both use pseudonyms—mine is *L_Hill* after author Laura Hillenbrand, who is a total CFS warrior like me, and his is *ChronicWarrior88*, although he hasn't said why. Was he born in '88? Is it his favorite number? I've no clue.

What I do know is the man. His essence. His soul. We've connected on everything from the music we like to listen to, to our shared passion for the show *The White Lotus* and all its truly horrible characters, to how many marshmallows you should add to your hot chocolate. Three is the answer, by the way, because two is too few and four is way too many.

And Warrior agrees.

So really, as far as I'm concerned, we know everything about each other that matters—marshmallows in hot chocolate included. What his actual name is and what he looks like feels immaterial at this point.

"Warrior thinks it's fantastic that I'm taking the job. He says he's a hockey fan and went to some of the Ice Breaker games here in town."

Her eyebrows ping up to meet her hairline. "He's local?"

"He lives in Portland."

"You know, Portland isn't that far away. You could go for a visit," she leads.

The thought has my heart beating harder in my chest, which of course my friend picks up on immediately.

"Clara, what's the point of this guy if you're not going to actually meet him?"

I shrug, feeling ridiculous. "I don't know."

The fact of the matter is I'm not ready to meet Warrior, even if he might turn out to be my dream guy. Chatting online, enjoying our easy companionship, sharing parts of my life with him, feels easy. Safe. I've only ever loved one man in my life, and when he left me and the kids, I felt like my world had ended.

The idea of opening myself up fully and completely again after all this time is terrifying.

"You can't hide behind a computer screen all your life, chatting with some guy you've never met, you know."

I lift my coffee and take a sip. "Sure, I can."

Bailey shakes her head at me and opens her mouth to reply when Ashlyn Thompkins appears beside our table, looking gorgeous in a pair of jeans and a pink shirt, her jacket draped across her arm.

"Hey, girls. How are my favorite childhood neighbors?" she says with a smile, her light brown hair in a messy bun, her gorgeous green eyes shining.

"You're back in town, Ashlyn?" Bailey asks, bouncing out of her seat and giving her a quick hug.

"Just for a while," she replies.

"Ashlyn's staying with her parents next door," I tell Bailey.

"Just like old times, then," Bailey replies. "Have you two been playing in the treehouse much?"

"Of course we have. We've had at least three tea parties there this week, right, Clara?" Ashlyn says, and I laugh.

"We sure knew how to live back then," I say.

"That might be true, but I tell you something: this town does not change one little bit," Ashlyn says, looking around the store.

"Sure, it does. We got a new teacher at the elementary school a few years back, and we got a new stop sign at the top of Main

Street. And don't forget these key lime cupcakes Neesha's making," I say, holding it up. "They're delicious, by the way."

Ashlyn laughs. "Maple Falls is rivaling LA for dynamism and excitement, I see."

"Would you like to join us?" I offer.

"Another time. I'm on a mission right now. Just popped in for coffee," she replies. "See you both soon." She flashes us her smile and saunters away.

"I haven't seen her in years," Bailey says. "You two were close back in the day."

"We were. It's nice to have her back." I take a bite of my cupcake and let out a sigh at the sweet lime-iness of it. "Oh, this is so good. We'll have to tell Neesha."

"Hey, who's that guy talking to Benny?" Bailey asks.

"What guy?" I ask around my mouthful, and I snap my attention across the store to see Benny talking with a big guy who's leaning down, listening to whatever it is Benny is telling him.

Immediately, with my mom-spidey senses on high alert, I leap out of my seat and scramble over to the comic section.

"...but why doesn't he fight back?" Benny is asking the man, who I notice is young enough to be about my age, give or take, and is looking intently at my son as though he's actually deeply involved in the conversation, not just humoring him.

"Because his powers get captured by Xerces, who's keeping them in an iron box held deep within the mountain," the man replies, as though that's a perfectly normal sentence to come out of a fully grown man's mouth.

I clear my throat as I slide my hands protectively over Benny's shoulders.

"Oh, hi, Mommy," Benny says, glancing at me momentarily before he returns his attention to his comic book—and the man.

"What are you guys talking about?" I ask lightly, narrowing my eyes at the man, my subtext being *who are you and why the heck are you talking with my son?*

The man shifts his attention from Benny to me, and as he does, he rises to his full height, all six feet whatever. He's tall, way taller than me, and, I admit begrudgingly, he's handsome. With his sandy blond hair kinda scruffy and a touch too long in that effortless, I-woke-up-handsome kind of way, his strong jawline is covered in a cropped beard with a few specks of salt and pepper that somehow works on him. My guess is he's mid-thirties, maybe older, and he's got the kind of face that makes your stomach do a slow flip.

In fact, he looks a little like a blond Jacob Elordi, as well as… familiar.

Yeah, definitely familiar.

"You must be Benny's mom," he says, his voice deep and sonorous, his gray eyes pinning me in place.

I tighten my hold on Benny's shoulders, lifting my chin in a vain attempt to appear taller than my five feet three inches against this…this…handsome *giant*. A handsome giant who thinks it's okay to talk with young boys they don't know in bookstores.

"I am Benny's mom. And you are?" I ask pointedly.

His ludicrously handsome face morphs into a smile as he extends one of his huge hands toward me. "Cade Lennox. Pleased to meet you, ma'am."

Ma'am? Oh, no, he did not just ma'am me!

How old does this guy think I *am*?

I'm too busy gaping at him to respond, and after a beat, he pulls his hand away, giving me a sheepish smile.

"I was talking with Benny here about the latest comic in the *The Timekeeper Chronicles*. We're both fans," he explains. "It's great that this bookstore gets the comics. I'm new in town and this is a big find for me. I thought I'd have to order them online, which just isn't the same."

"Well, that's very nice of you, Mr.—" I'm about to say "Elordi" when it snaps into place who this guy is. He's the right winger for the newly minted Ice Breakers. In fact, I've got a picture of him in his New York City Blades uniform in my spreadsheet at home. His most recent season stats float before my eyes. Thirty-seven goals, twenty-four assists, average slap-shot over 100 mph, and forty-two penalty minutes, mostly for chirping at refs, which he has a reputation for doing.

"Lennox," he finishes for me, shooting me a look that seems to ask whether my brain is functioning properly.

"I just worked out who you are."

"Because I told you who I am already?" he asks, his eyes dancing, and there's something in his tone that has me narrowing my gaze.

Wait. Is this guy *flirting* with me?

"You know, just before, when I said my name is Cade Lennox." He waggles his brows playfully.

Oh, yes, he's definitely flirting with me. And in front of Benny, too! Does this guy have no boundaries? No shame?

And then it all falls into place.

My research went beyond player stats and into their personal lives, and my research on this guy told me that Cade Lennox is not only a talented winger who's helped his team make it to the playoffs three years running, but he is the biggest hockey-playing womanizer to walk the earth.

And with the reputation a lot of these hockey players seem to have, that's saying something.

I extend my hand to shake his, channeling my inner business-woman. As he takes my hand in his, his large hand completely dwarfs my own, making me feel even smaller.

"I'm Clara Johnson, social media manager for the Ice Break-ers. Or at least I will be on Monday."

My eyes drop momentarily to his T-shirt, which has an image of one of the characters from Benny's favorite comic book series.

Huh. He's a womanizing hockey player who looks like a blond Jacob Elordi and wears comic book T-shirts like he's a character on *The Big Bang Theory*? Talk about a dichotomy.

"I guess that means we'll be working together," he says.

I press my lips together, doing my best to ignore the way the combination of his gaze and the warmth of his hand is making my pulse quicken. "That's right."

"Cool," he replies, his lips pulling into an easy smile.

"Cool," I repeat, wishing I could come up with something more, well, more like what an actual adult would say.

But it's hard to think straight when someone as attractive as Cade Lennox is holding your hand in his and looking at you with those gray eyes, looming over you, all big and…there.

It's *a lot*.

But he's a womanizing professional hockey player. And I'm a *ma'am*.

The thought is enough to snap me out of whatever this thing is between us.

Benny twists his head to look up at me. "Mommy, you've gone pink. Are you hot?"

I don't look at Cade Lennox.

"I'm fine, Benny. Say goodbye to Mr. Lennox and come have a cupcake with Bailey."

"But I want to get this comic book," he whines.

"I'll get it for you after," I grind out.

"Promise?"

"Promise."

"Hey, great to meet you, Benny. And remember, Zara Kazan is the true hero of the series. Or rather, the true heroine," Cade Lennox says to my son.

"Nah-uh. It's Max Griffin. Everyone knows that," Benny insists.

"Let's go," I say, and as I lead Benny to the table, I take a quick look back at the guy, only to see him smiling at me, his eyes lit up with playfulness like a string of fairy lights.

And my dang belly gives a little flip.

CHAPTER 4
CADE

I LET the hot water run down my back, washing away the pain in my side following my collision with Weston Smith out on the ice in our first ever team practice. He's from the minors, the Tennessee Wolves to be precise, and the guy sure has something to prove, slamming me unnecessarily hard against the plexiglass during one of our plays.

At least I know he'll be effective in defense when it comes to an actual game.

I rub my side. Yup, *real effective.*

It didn't help that Coach Hauser had already put us through a bunch of bruising drills beforehand. Coach is tough, tougher than my last coach, who I was pretty sure had some kind of grudge against hockey players. But he got results.

This guy? I bet he'll get them, too.

It doesn't hurt that he's got a group of players all wanting to make their mark on the newest team in the League. And I count myself in that equation.

One thing I can say is it's great to have my former Blades team captain leading us. Jamie Hayes always sets the tone for the team: work hard and have each other's backs out on the ice, no matter what. I know how he ticks, what he expects from his men, and I'm here for it, one hundred percent.

I picture the other guys in the team as I wash the sweat from my hair.

Carson Crane, nicknamed "Bama" because he originates from the state, has talent sparking off of him out on the ice. I've come up against him a bunch of times on the Blades, and the guy has killer instincts on the ice. He'll be a good teammate, and much better on my team than against me.

Canadian Asher Tremblay has an ever-present smile, Asher's easy to get along with, and he's taken me up on my open invitation to the guys to lift weights in my fully equipped garage gym later this week. He seems like the kind of guy I could click with, and it'd be good to make a friend in this new town.

Defenseman Lucian Lowe is quiet and a little intense, and I know it'll take a while to get to know him. But he seems like a good guy, and he's an excellent player, one I'm more than happy to have on the team. He's different than his counterpart, Weston Smith, who, when he's not smashing me against the boards, loves to crack a joke, and with a bunch of jocks, there's always an opportunity for humor.

Then there's that French guy, Clément Rivière, nicknamed Frenchie for obvious reasons. Of course, I know him by reputation from his time on the Les Lions de Paris team where he made his mark, and he sure comes across as your stereotypical French guy, all suave and dramatic with his accented English.

My mind turns to the perky blonde with the pretty blue eyes in her jeans and white T-shirt I met over the comics in the bookstore on Main Street. She had on a long gray cardigan that reached down to her knees, skimming her womanly figure. And what a figure. Slim but nowhere near skinny, with rounded hips and curves where they're meant to be.

Hey, I'm a guy. I noticed.

She had a practically makeup-free face but for something glossy on her lips, her blonde shoulder-length hair in soft waves.

In a world full of puck bunnies, I'm not used to meeting women who aren't fully made-up, without a hair out of place, their assets on full display.

Clara Johnson was…refreshing. Yeah, refreshing is the word. Refreshing and totally hot.

And it was as clear as day that she had next to zero interest in me. In fact, the way she grabbed a hold of her son when she first arrived told me she thought I was some kind of weird predator with an ulterior motive.

I'll admit, while I was checking her out, my eyes did flick briefly to her left hand, and you know what? No ring. That's right, I "ma'amed" a single mom who's probably only about my age. Nah, scrub that. I "ma'amed" a *hot* single mom who's probably only about my age.

Man, I bet she *loved* that.

The truth is I've been addicted to comic books ever since I was Benny's age, which I pick at about eight or nine. Back then, comics were my escape. I would take my weekly pocket money Mom gave me to the comic store in our small town and carefully select which one I got to take home. Mom would always roll her eyes in a good-natured way, knowing how much I loved that world of superheroes and villains, and the good guys always winning in the end.

So different from the world I lived in.

The bad guy definitely won there.

And I still hate him for it.

I squirt some shampoo into the palm of my hand and lather up as my jaw twitches as I think of my father, the man who put the word absent in *absent father figure*. The man who would only turn up once every couple years with some sob story, treat my mom like a piece of dirt beneath his shoe, and then leave again.

I never understood why she let him back in, time and time again. But let him in she did, whenever he would turn up on our stoop, believing his lame excuse as to why he hadn't been around, why he had no money to give her to support his own kids, giving her some cock and bull story about whatever it was that he knew would get him back into our lives.

At first, I was excited to see him, just the way Mom was. He was my dad, and he'd come back to us. I'd try to spend as much time with him as I could, inviting him to my hockey games, telling him all about my friends and my comic collection, eager to have father-son time. And he'd come to a couple games, making my heart soar, then he'd get involved with something— or someone—else and drift away, until one day he wouldn't be home when I got back from school.

Then, as I grew older and his visits grew farther and farther apart, I began to resent him. Who did he think he was, coming into our lives whenever he wanted, and then disappearing again?

So, I made the decision long ago that I wasn't going to treat people like he did. When—if—I ever settled down, it would be forever. I wouldn't jerk either my wife or my kids around like he had done.

There's no freaking way I'll ever be like him.

But a big part of me was afraid I would turn into him. So, I steered clear of commitment, kept my relationships short and shallow. And it worked for a while. I didn't have a wife and kids I was messing around. I could be whatever I wanted to be, and the League afforded me the ability to do as I pleased, no strings attached.

In the end, that lifestyle wasn't the answer.

Sure, the women I dated knew the score from the get-go. I was there for a good time, not a long time, and they got that. But, do that for long enough and your soul grows weary.

Now I've become a man who wants to fall in love for the very first time.

And I guess that could start with *not* flirting with women like Clara Johnson.

No matter how much I want to.

"Yo, Lennox. You done yet?" Asher calls out.

"What's it to you?"

"Coach wants us in the locker room to meet some dude about marketing, so get your butt out here."

"Be there in two." I push the conundrum of Clara Johnson and the new me from my mind as I rinse off the shampoo and then switch the water off. Immediately, I miss the therapeutic heat.

Man, I'm not as young as I once was.

And yeah, even *thinking* that makes me feel old.

I might not quite be Jamie's age, but at thirty-three I don't bounce back from the brutality of the sport like I once did. And hockey has got to be the most brutal sport of all, except maybe rugby. Those guys are insane.

Although I'm not in that headspace yet, sometime soon I know I'm going to have to think about what comes after hockey.

Which is all the more reason to get on with the new me.

I grab a towel and dry myself off before I wrap it around my waist, slicking my hair back. I pad across the cold tile floor out into the locker room. I'm expecting to see a rabble of guys in various stages of undress, talking and laughing as they get ready to head home after practice.

What I see is every single one of my teammates fully dressed in their regular clothes, sitting in front of their lockers, looking at a woman speaking. I swivel around to see who they're listening to only to capture the gaze of the hot mom I ma'amed yesterday.

Clara Johnson. The woman I've just told myself I'm *not* going to flirt with.

Her eyes slide quickly down to my abs and back up again, and within seconds her cheeks begin to flush, and she pulls her gaze from me, focusing back on my teammates.

I glance down at my bare, glistening chest, my towel wrapped low around my waist—not exactly the kind of attire that doesn't attract attention. But it wasn't like I planned this. Asher told me some guy wanted to talk with us, not Clara. And how was I to know everyone else would be dressed already?

I make my way to my locker and take my seat.

"Dude, did you know you're just in a towel?" Weston stage whispers to my left.

"Yeah, thanks, I got that," I say back with a roll of my eyes.

"So, I'm looking for volunteers," Clara says, and although I've got no idea what she wants volunteers for, I raise my hand along with Weston and Asher.

Despite my new leaf being turned here in Maple Falls, I'd like to spend some more time with this hot, gorgeous woman who doesn't seem to like me—but who blushes at the sight of my bare chest.

Yeah, I kind of liked that.

Clara's eyes glide over me once more as she lifts her lips into a smile. "Awesome. Thanks, guys. Stay behind and we can chat about the campaign, okay?"

"You got it," Asher responds.

"Campaign?" I say under my breath to Weston.

"Social media. Weren't you listening? No, wait, you were still in the shower getting close and personal with a bar of soap," he replies with a smirk.

"Whatever," I say, returning my attention to Clara, a much prettier prospect than my teammate.

Man, she's so pretty in a total girl-next-door kind of way, with her porcelain skin and full lips. She's not in her mom outfit today, but rather something more professional: a pencil skirt that does everything for her curvaceous hips, and a pale blue cotton shirt that enhances the blue of her eyes. Her blonde hair is tied up in a low bun, and I can't help but imagine loosening her hair to see it fall in soft waves, like the way she looked at the bookstore.

Geez, stop.

I can't go thinking about her in that way. I'm here to clean up my rep, get a new start as the man I want to be. And what do I do? Start fantasizing about the first girl I've met.

"Thank you, Ms. Johnson. I'm sure all the guys will help you out with these campaigns over the coming weeks and months," Coach Hauser says. "Isn't that right, men?"

"Yes, Coach," I say along with the rest of the team.

"You're free to go. Back here seven sharp tomorrow," Coach says.

And then the guys start to collect their things and leave, and I throw on a pair of jeans, and a T-shirt, ready to meet with Clara and the other two in the players' lounge, adjacent to the locker room.

A couple of the guys are already in there watching some old footage of a game, so the four of us sit at the other end of the room on some comfy sofas by the coffee machine.

Clara's back is as straight as a rod, her hands clasped on her lap, and I wonder if she's nervous. "First of all, thank you all for volunteering for this campaign. Everyone on the team will get the chance to work on one or more of these, but it's great to start small with just the three of you."

"Sure thing, Ms. Johnson. Anything you want," Weston says with a grin.

"Yeah, we got you," Asher adds.

"That's great, guys. Please call me Clara. I'm probably about your age and I'm new at all this. So…yeah." She lifts her lips in a smile.

Yup, definitely nervous.

"You're Asher Tremblay," she says, pointing at him. "And you're Weston Smith."

"That's right. You're a quick study." Asher flashes her a smile, and I'm not sure if he's interested in Clara or he just likes everybody.

"And I'm Cade Lennox," I add when she doesn't refer to me. "Even though you already know that since we've already met."

"Wait, what?" Weston asks, his gaze darting between us.

"Yeah, we go way back. Right, Clara?" I say, throwing her a wink.

I'm being friendly, *not* flirty. It's all good.

She gives me what I can only refer to as her *stern mom* look, and I immediately regret the wink. That's the old Cade, not the new and improved version, even if I'm just teasing her, having a bit of fun. What can I say? It's a reflex action around a beautiful woman.

And it's probably partly what got me the reputation I'm now trying to shrug off.

"Mr. Lennox and I met in the bookstore while I was buying a comic book for my son," she explains to the others.

"Hitting on a mom? *Dude*," Weston says, judging me.

"It wasn't like that. Benny's a cool kid. We got to talking about *The Timekeeper Chronicles*," I say.

"The what now?" Asher asks.

He hasn't heard of *The Timekeeper Chronicles*?

"The comics? The game? The *movie*?" When they all give me blank looks, I say, "What planet do you live on?" I point at my chest. I'm wearing a T-shirt that reads *Ask me about my temporal paradox* above *The Timekeepers Chronicles* logo.

Asher shrugs. "I thought that was just some quote of yours you liked so much you got it screen-printed onto a shirt."

Weston snort laughs and the two men bump fists.

I ignore them, instead asking Clara, "What exactly do you want us to do?" I shoot her a smile that I hope tells her I'm not the creep she thinks I am.

Man, this is what my life has become?

"My boss, Veronica Reynolds, thought we should kick things off with some dances on the ice." The look on her face suggests this is not her first choice.

"Awesome!" Weston says.

"I'm a trained dancer," Asher adds with a smirk.

My eyebrows ping upwards. "You are?"

"Yeah." He stands up and busts out some quick moves to prove his point, and I'll admit, he looks like he knows what he's doing.

"Where did you learn to do that, man?" Weston asks.

"Dance school, dummy," he replies as he returns to his seat.

"That's amazing! I'm so glad you volunteered for this campaign," Clara says, clearly impressed. "Can you dance on the ice?"

"Is water wet?" he asks.

"Sure is!" Weston replies enthusiastically.

"In that case, let's see what you've got out on the ice," Clara surprises us all by saying as she rises to her feet.

"What, now?" Asher asks.

She shrugs. "Why not?"

"Sure. Give me ten minutes to suit up," Asher replies, jumping to his feet.

"You're not Iron Man, dude," I say with a laugh.

"Oh yeah? Wait until you see me out there," he responds, and he and Weston make their way back toward the locker room.

"You coming, Lennox?" Weston calls, turning to look at us as he walks backwards.

"Be there in a sec," I call back. "Kids, huh?" I say to Clara as the two guys disappear around the corner, only stopping to high five the guys watching the TV.

"How old do you think I *am*?" she asks, her brows pulled together.

Well, that one backfired.

"I didn't mean I was just making a joke."

"A joke? Okay."

"Sorry."

She waves my apology away with a flick of her wrist. "It's fine. And I'm thirty-one, in case you wanted to know."

"Huh," I reply, doing a quick calculation in my head.

"What does that mean?"

"Benny's what? Seven or eight?"

"He's eight."

"You had him young."

"My daughter's ten," she says, lifting her chin as though to challenge me.

"*Real* young," I amend with a smile that I'm hoping will disarm her.

Not to boast, but I have been told my smile is disarming.

Her features relax a touch.

Heck, yeah. The famous Lennox smile strikes again.

"You're right, Cade. I did have my kids young."

"And their dad? I noticed you're not wearing a ring."

Yeah, I'm fishing. Don't judge. The new me can still fish.

"Their dad is a few years older than me," she replies with a smug smile.

Touché, Clara Johnson. Touché.

I guess that'll teach me to get personal.

We stand in silence for a beat before she gestures at the exit to the locker room. "Aren't you going to 'make like Iron Man,' too?"

"Make like Iron Man? Oh, you mean get into my game day gear? Sure. I just wanted to take this chance to say I was sorry for…well, I'm just sorry."

She gives me a brittle smile. "I got that. Thanks."

It's hard to tell from her tone if she's being sarcastic or not. I decide to go with *not* because the way I see it, life's too short to get hung up on the small stuff, and I much prefer to take people at face value than suspect them of ulterior motives.

"I'll go get changed, but I warn you, I'm no dancer," I tell her.

She smiles at me. "We'll see about that."

I guess we will.

CHAPTER 5
CLARA

WHAT AM I DOING?

I promised myself I wouldn't film any cheesy, overdone dancing hockey players when I took this job, and what am I doing right this very moment? Filming three super big guys, wearing all their game day gear, dancing to that catchy Rosé and Bruno Mars' song "APT" like a bunch of overly energetic teenage kids in *High School Musical*. It's cheesier than a bowl of mac and cheese slathered in extra Edam.

Yup, first day of my job and this is my life now.

But you know what? Today isn't proving to be as intimidating as I feared it might. Veronica has been so nice and helpful, and the marketing assistant, Millie, has gotten me coffee, helped me set up my desk, and shown me how to use the computer system. Even the big boss, CEO Paul Vaughn, who's answerable only to Troy Hart, the team owner, welcomed me with a warm smile, even if he went on to call me Claire.

Sure, it was intimidating to walk into the team's locker room post-practice with Coach Hauser and get confronted with all those huge, athletic, brawny guys who sail across the ice as though they weigh less than five pounds, when in reality they weigh something like *two hundred* and five.

And when Cade Lennox sauntered in late, wearing nothing but a towel? That nearly threw me off my stride completely, his super broad shoulders, shapely arms, defined pecs covered in a light dusting of hair, and the obligatory taut washboard abs on display.

Not that I was looking.

Okay. I was totally looking.

But anyone would. The guy looks like Jacob Elordi and Thor had a love child, threw on a load more muscle, and gave him crazy talent on the ice.

Besides, we all know you don't get to play professional hockey in the NHL unless you're in peak physical shape, and Cade Lennox is certainly that.

And then I remembered that he thinks I'm an overprotective mom of at least forty-five who he saw fit to flirt with right in front of my son, and I'd managed to pull my gaze from all his hotness with relative ease.

Since then, of course, he's apologized, and as used to female attention as his reputation suggests he is, it seemed genuine enough.

I know it'll be useful in my job if I can get on well with all the players, Cade Lennox included. I plan on working with them for my various social media initiatives over the coming season, and they're more likely to be helpful if we have a cordial working relationship.

Cordial. Good word. That's what I'll aim for with Cade Lennox. Cordial and professional and in no way regarding him as a handsome hockey player with an incredible, honed physique, and all that sexy manliness that seems to ooze out of his every pore.

I clear my throat.

It's a work in progress.

Perhaps having an online relationship with a man I've never seen in real life means I'm missing out on some of the important parts of human connection. If what Warrior and I have is, strictly speaking, a "relationship." But I definitely feel an emotional connection with him. I wouldn't go so far as to say it's love, but it sure feels…nice. Easy. He gets me and I get him.

Besides, everyone knows that one of the key aspects of a romantic relationship is an emotional connection and affection. I have those with Warrior. Just not the actual being able to see him part.

I definitely don't have that issue with the three big Ice Breakers in their bulky game day uniforms in front of me on the ice right now. Asher Tremblay, Weston Smith, and Cade Lennox are standing together on the ice, trying out the dance moves Asher is demonstrating for them—to varying degrees of success.

By which I mean Weston and Cade look like oversized newborn deer trying to walk for the first time next to Asher's smooth, confident dance moves.

I'm playing the catchy tune on my phone so they get their moves in sync with the beat, and I'll overlay it with the song when I upload it to social media.

"No, man, it's like this," Asher is saying to the other two as he lifts his foot and taps it with his gloved hand, then does the same to the other foot before spinning around, his arms above his head.

I applaud him from my spot at the team bench as I lean over the boards for a clear shot. "That was awesome, Asher!"

He smiles at me before he returns to the lesson, and I watch once more as Cade and Weston do their best to copy Asher's moves.

I try not to laugh. Really, I do. But they look so dang funny next to Asher's sleek, honed dance skills, even the looks on their faces showing they're completely flummoxed by this new way of moving on the ice.

"Just bend your knees a little more," Asher instructs, and Cade and Weston follow suit. "There you go! Now swing your hips to the right, arms up, and...awesome! Now watch this."

Asher glides backward across the ice, his movements fluid despite being in full hockey gear. The Canadian's ever-present smile widens as he executes a series of coordinated arm movements that have absolutely no business looking that graceful on skates. According to Asher, this is a trending TikTok dance, only right now it looks more like a gem from a blooper reel.

I make sure I capture everything on my phone.

"Come on, man. I look like I'm having a seizure," Weston complains.

"Nah, you're doing great, Smith!" Asher says, not missing a beat. "It's all in the hips. It's just like you're trying to dodge a check, but make it sexy, eh?"

I snort laugh and am glad the guys are too engrossed in their dance routine to notice.

"Make it sexy? Dude, I'm wearing thirty pounds of protective gear and sweating like I just did suicide drills," Cade complains.

"No one wants to hear about your sweat, Lennox," Weston says, and he receives a shove from Cade.

"Yeah, sweat isn't sexy," Asher says before he transitions into the next move. "This is the move that gets all the likes. Just watch, okay?"

There really is something so endearing about watching some of the NHL's top players trying to nail a dance move that's probably meant for lithe teenagers with very different builds than these guys.

Cade and Weston copy Asher, looking about as comfortable

as a couple of cats in a room of cucumbers. Despite knowing I shouldn't, I can't help but zoom in on Cade. His usual easy confidence is replaced by a look of intense focus, his brows pulled together in concentration. His dark blond hair is curling under his helmet, and when he flicks his eyes in my direction, I quickly zoom my phone back out.

Professional distance. That's what I need here.

"Lennox, you're thinking too much. Less hockey brain, more boy band," Asher scolds.

"More *boy band*?" Cade asks with a note of distaste. "I don't even have a single boy band neuron, let alone a whole brain."

"Asher's right. Channel your best Justin Timberlake," Weston says. "Like me." He busts out a move that's really not bad.

"With those looks you've got total boy band potential," Asher says, clapping Cade on the back.

Cade shakes his head, grinning before his eyes flash to mine once more, sending an unexpected flutter through my chest.

Weston attempts the hip shake again and nearly topples over, saved only by Cade's quick reflexes as he grabs his teammate's elbow.

"Give me a brutal game against the Nebraska Knights over this any day of the week," Weston grumbles.

"I'm starting to think you suggested this just to watch us make fools of ourselves," Cade calls out to me.

"You volunteered, remember?" I shoot back, willing that weird flutter to die. "And besides, Coach Hauser told me the winner gets out of something called 'bag skate' tomorrow."

Both Weston and Cade straighten up.

"You didn't mention this is a competition," Asher says.

"There's no way I want a bag skate," Cade adds, resuming the position Asher put him in a moment ago. "Let's do this. Bring on the boy band brain!"

I press my lips together to stifle a laugh. "This is gold, guys. The fans are going to love seeing this side of you."

"You're filming this?" Cade asks in surprise.

"Of course I am," I reply. "It's my job."

"I thought you were only filming the dance, not us bickering like a pack of old women," he replies, and then thinks better of it. "Not that old women do bicker."

This time I can't stop the laughter from bursting free.

"You're such an idiot," Weston says, clocking Cade on his helmeted head with his gloved hand.

Cade shrugs. "I'm just trying to be PC."

"Line up, guys. Let's give the full dance a shot," Asher instructs.

They line up facing me, and as I start the song over they begin by shrugging one shoulder, then the other, then swaying from side to side, and when Rosé's voice sounds out, they break into three and begin to follow the moves Asher taught them. It's all going perfectly until Cade moves to the left instead of the right and bangs right into Weston.

"Wrong way, man!" Weston yells and all three of them come to a stop.

"Keep going!" I call out over the music, because who knows? Maybe hockey players messing up dance moves will be the next TikTok trend?

The guys resume their routine, picking up where they left off, and with only one minor mishap—Weston tapping the wrong foot—they finish, and I cut the music.

"I know we can do better, Clara. Take it from the top?" Asher says.

"Sure thing." I start the song again, and this time the guys do the routine flawlessly, and clearly have fun doing it, their burgeoning team chemistry obvious in the video.

"That's a wrap," I tell them when I'm certain I've got the footage I need.

The guys skate across the ice toward me.

Asher says, "I'm happy to help choreograph any of your other dance videos, Clara. Just say the word."

"That's so sweet of you, Asher. I'll definitely take you up on that," I reply.

No matter how much I may want to pursue other initiatives, Management has made it clear they want dance videos so Asher's skills will come in handy. And, if I'm being totally honest, I've enjoyed it.

"How about we do another one now?" Cade suggests. "Got any other ideas, Tremblay?"

"So many ideas," he replies with a grin. "We did this one when I was with the Renegades where we lined up behind the lead and stuck our sticks out so it looked like he had multiple sticks before we broke out and skated around. It looked awesome on video."

"I'll give that a shot," Cade says.

"Yeah, me too," Weston agrees.

I smile at the guys. They're all so willing to help. I don't know what I expected from them, but I thought I might need to at least use some persuasion. "Thank you. This helps a lot."

"Wait," Cade says as the other two turn to skate off. "Don't you think our social media expert should join us?"

Immediately, I hold my hands up in the air. "No way. I'm just the videographer today, and besides, you guys are doing great. You don't need me."

But my protest falls on deaf ears as Cade grins, saying, "Come on, Clara. Where's your team spirit?" His eyes are dancing, trained on me, and once again those dang flutters claim my chest.

"I'm not dressed for it," I say, gesturing at my pencil skirt and heels. I might have thrown a warm jacket on over my office-appropriate attire when we came out to the rink, but there's no way it's skating-appropriate.

"You want some pads and a helmet?" Cade asks with a cheeky look on his face. "Come on. I'll be right there to catch you if you fall."

I swallow as an image of me being held in Cade's big arms flashes before my eyes.

"I'm in high heels, which aren't exactly ice-friendly," I reply, as though that can't be fixed by a pair of arena-owned skates I myself used to rent out to the public in one of my many, many jobs.

"I'm sure that's not a problem, right, Asher?" Cade asks as the other two glide across the ice to rejoin us.

"Not a problem whatsoever," Asher agrees.

"Who will film it? There's no one here but us," I protest.

Yup, I'm grasping at straws here. The last thing I want is to be recorded as part of some TikTok dance routine on the ice. It's not exactly in my job description. And the thought of being that close to Cade? Nope. Not happening.

"It's a nice idea, Cade, but it looks like we'll have to do it some other time. If at all," I say.

"Hey!" Cade calls out and a young guy in a dark blue boiler suit I hadn't noticed before looks over at us.

"Me?" he calls back.

"Can you do us a solid?"

"Anything for the legendary Cade Lennox," the guy replies, jogging over to us. It's then that I recognize him as Joel Fincher, a kid I used to babysit back when I was fourteen. Not that he's a kid anymore.

"See? Problem solved," Cade says to me with a satisfied grin.

I push out a breath. This guy sure is persistent when he wants something.

Joel arrives at the players' bench and it's clear he's completely starstruck by the guys, punching their gloved hands and grinning like he won the lottery.

"Hey, Clara," he says to me, barely tearing his gaze from the players.

"Hi, Joel."

"This is for the Ice Breaker's TikTok, right?" Joel asks.

"Sure," I reply, because isn't that obvious? Why else would I have three hockey players dancing on the ice for me?

Don't answer that.

"Got it," Joel replies, grinning so hard he's at risk of splitting his face in two.

"Okay, let's do this!" Asher declares, and Cade pulls the door open, offering me his gloved hand.

I open my mouth to protest, but I'm all out of excuses.

I may as well get this over with.

With the reluctance of a kid going to the dentist, I take Cade's proffered gloved hand and step gingerly onto the ice, instantly regretting my heels and skirt combo. But then to be fair to me, I didn't think my first day on the job as Social Media Manager for the Ice Breakers would involve me taking part in a TikTok dance with three of the players.

Go figure.

Asher demonstrates the dance I just filmed, and as I clutch onto Cade's hand for support, I try my best not to slip off and fall flat on my face as I move my feet in sync with the guys. Despite the fact I'm doing my best to concentrate on the steps, it's hard not to be hyperaware of Cade at my side.

"Oh, man, this is awesome!" Joel declares, holding my phone in his hands. "You guys look sick! Even you, Clara."

I let out a surprised laugh at Joel's comment when Asher calls, "And now turn!" and as I do my legs fly from underneath me, and my breath wooshes out as I scrunch my eyes shut, bracing for the impact of cold, hard ice against my poor, under-protected butt.

But the ice-cold contact fails to happen, and when my eyes spring open I see Cade, his eyes wide with alarm as large, strong arms pull me against his firm body.

He grins down at me as my heart beats out of my chest.

I tell myself it's because I almost fell, but being in Cade's arms feels…well, it feels pretty dang amazing.

Not that I'm going to tell *him* that.

"Thanks," I mumble, the heat rising in my cheeks as I gaze up at him, at total odds with the cold of the arena.

"My pleasure," he replies, and the way he says those two words sends a flash of something hot through me that I've got to work hard at resisting.

But resist it I must, no matter how good this feels.

I haven't been held by a man since Dwayne left me for my friend. And that was years ago.

I heave out a breath as I drag my gaze from his. I need to remember that this guy is a total player, and I don't mean just on the ice. He probably catches falling women in his big, strong arms every day of the week—and I bet most of them don't even bother to resist the heat this feeling elicits.

But I'm not one of those women, and I refuse to act on my physical attraction for this man. There are so many reasons, the non-fraternization clause in my employment contract being right at the top of that list.

Throwing away my new job because I'm attracted to one of the players? Not going to happen.

"You guys, I'm getting so many likes on this!" Joel calls out.

Wait. *Likes?*

I snap my attention to Joel, who's still holding up my phone, pointing it straight at Cade and me. "Cade, would you mind putting me down? Like *now.*"

"I'll do you one better," he replies as he glides me smoothly back toward the bench, still holding me close in his arms. Holding me in one arm, he pulls open the door, and returns me to my feet—which I note are now trembling.

Argh!

But I've got a much bigger problem to deal with right now than trembling legs brought about by my inappropriate attraction to an oversized hockey player called Cade.

"What do you mean, likes, Joel?" I ask as I hold my hand out for my phone.

"On the livestream," he replies, and I almost blackout in shock.

"You livestreamed this?" I croak, my heart drumming in my ears. I snatch the phone away and hastily switch the recording off.

"That's what you wanted, right?" Joel replies, his eyes darting between me and Cade.

"Yeah, I'm not sure about that," Cade mumbles as he watches me.

I swallow, tension claiming my chest. What will Management think of me, dancing with the players on my first day and—worse, so much worse—landing in the arms of their star right winger, me gazing up at him as though to declare to the world that I've got a fat crush on Cade Lennox?

I just turned "strictly professional" into "romantically questionable" with one paltry slip on the ice—metaphorically as well as literally.

I close my eyes and suck in air, my chest buzzing. I will officially be the person to hold the unenviable position of the shortest-serving social media manager for an NHL team in the history of time. My dream job snatched away from me with a simple slip on the ice.

CHAPTER 6
CADE

I TAKE A BREATHER, my heart rate drumming as I gaze out the window at the trees punctuating the lush grass of my yard. The realtor who rented me this place told me I'd love the tranquility. At first, I thought the silence might drive me crazy. But now, as I look out at the trees with their leaves turning from shades of green to golds and oranges and reds, I get what she meant.

This place is good for the soul.

Yup, I've become *that* guy, the one who needs his *personal space* to *recharge*.

Maybe that's part of the new, more mature me? Or maybe I'm just enjoying being in this new town I call home.

"Lennox, you spotting me or what?" Jamie says, and I turn to see my team captain lying on the bench in my newly set up gym—the gym with the best view in all of Maple Falls.

I gave an open invitation to all the guys on the team at practice to use my gym, and today both Jamie Hayes and Carson "Bama" Crane have taken me up on the offer.

"How much you pressing today, Captain? Want to push those boundaries?" I ask as I position myself over his head.

Carson grunts as he pushes up from a squat, a crazy number of weights held on a bar across his shoulders. We both turn to watch him.

"Man, that's impressive, Crane," I say, but he's too busy concentrating on not being crushed by the massive weight to reply.

"Nah. Just the usual. I'm still sore from yesterday's practice. I'm convinced Coach Hauser is a sadist," Jamie says.

I flash him a smile. "That's because you're an old man these days, old man."

"Hey, less of the old. I've only got a year on you. Ready?"

I lift the weighted bar from its hooks and help to lower it down to Jamie's chest. "Got it?" I ask and he nods. I let go and watch as he pumps the iron with practiced precision, grunting with the exertion.

"You might be old, but you've still got it," I tell him.

When he gets to the end of his set, his face is red, perspiration beading on his forehead. He pulls himself up. "Okay. Your turn."

"Yes, Captain," I say with a small salute. I win a bat on the arm from him for my trouble.

"If only you'd show me that kind of deference on the ice."

"*Deference*? You swallowed a dictionary this morning?"

"It's a word," he replies.

"Yeah, I know it's a word. It's just not a word I've heard *you* use before."

"Me neither," says Carson before he chugs some water.

Jamie rolls his eyes. "Whatever. Assume the position, Lennox."

I chuckle as I lie down on the bench he just vacated, warm from his efforts, and get into position. Jamie spots me as I do my set, and by the time I'm done, I'm sweating as hard as he was, my muscles shaking from the effort.

"Nice form," my captain says. "Don't you think, Crane?"

"Looked good to me," Carson replies as he does a bicep curl.

"So, what do you think of the team?" Jamie asks as I pull off my damp T-shirt that was sticking to me and towel myself down. I collect my water bottle and take a much-needed swig of water.

I wipe the sweat from my forehead with the towel. "I think it's gonna take some time for us to learn to work together, but there's a lot of talent." I turn to Carson. "I'm glad you're on my team these days, Crane. No offense, but when we used to come up against you on the Blades, I hated you."

"None taken," he replies. "I hated you, too."

And I can't help but smile at the image of the great winger sitting on a unicorn.

"Yeah, it's weird when you're playing against a guy one day and the next you gotta play nice when you're on the same team. But that's the League, my friends," Jamie says. "How are you finding the move to this small town? Hallmark movie enough for you?"

I laugh. "You got that right. My mom loves Hallmark movies, particularly around the holidays. The first thing she said when I told her I was moving here to Maple Falls is that I might find a local girl and fall in love."

"Never say never," Jamie replies.

My mind instantly turns to Clara Johnson and the way she felt in my arms the other day on the ice. The way her blue-eyed gaze captured mine, her full lips forming a surprised "o." It would have been so easy to lean down and brush a soft kiss against those lips. So easy.

It was a total Hallmark movie moment.

"I like it here," Bama ekes out mid bicep curl.

"Me, too. This place is the total opposite of Manhattan, but it's growing on me," I say.

"Yeah," Jamie replies with a laugh. "We've gone from millions of people to what? A few thousand?"

"Ten thousand, I think. Or eleven?" I reply.

"Whatever the number, it's a shock to the system to have all this nature everywhere, right?" He gestures at the view. "That's a lot of trees."

"I like 'em," Carson says, returning his hand weights to the stack.

I smile at him. "Yeah, me too. It's peaceful."

"Who's being an old guy now?" Jamie asks with a sardonic laugh.

"I'm going to get a refill in the kitchen," Carson says, holding up his water bottle.

Once he's out of earshot, Jamie asks, "Do you think it'll do what you want it to do?"

"What, the nature?" I ask.

He shakes his head. "Nah, I mean the move here to small town USA, away from the temptations of the big city."

Being my long-time teammate and friend, Jamie is one of the few people in my inner circle, and I trust him implicitly. He was there for my partying days, when I would change the woman on my arm more often than I would change my socks, and he was there when that lifestyle lost its lure for me.

He knows I leapt at the chance to be on this newly minted NHL team for a bunch of reasons, but right there at the top of the list was to leave that world well and truly behind.

I take a seat on the bench and let out a breath. "You know my reasons for being here."

"Yup."

"And you know how much I need to reinvent myself."

"Yup."

"The thing is, I met a girl." I twist my mouth as I wait for the inevitable to follow.

"What the heck? What are talking about? You met a girl? Have you learned *nothing*?"

And there it is.

"I know, I know," I say with a shrug, my palms up. "But this one's different. Trust me."

"She's got a long tail and green scales?"

"She's still human, dude," I say with a shake of my head.

"Go on. Spill. Who is she?"

"You know the social media manager for the team?"

"You mean the blonde? What's her name? Claire?"

"Clara," I correct. "Clara Johnson."

"You've got a thing for someone we work with? Lennox—" he warns, but I cut him off.

"It's not like that. I'm the new me. I'm not interested in some fling with the woman. I...like her."

"Because she's hot."

"No. Because she's funny and sassy and speaks her mind. I like that in a woman."

"And she's hot."

"Okay. I admit, she's hot. I'm a guy. Of course I'm gonna like that about her."

He chews on his lip, assessing me.

"What are you thinking? You're freaking me out right now."

"I'm thinking that you're a total freaking idiot. That's what I'm thinking."

"Don't pussy foot around the topic, Captain," I reply.

"Remind me because I'm not sure my memory serves me all that well on this, but didn't you hook up with...let me think... the owner of the Blades's *daughter*?"

He's right. I did do that. And it did not end well.

Misty was cute and fun and hot—of course—and she told me

she wanted a no-strings fling with what she called the "playboy" of the team. And stupid me, I thought she meant it. So, I did what most guys would do when they meet a hot woman promising a no-strings affair, and I went for it.

Sadly for me it turned out that Misty's idea of no-strings and the rest of the world's idea bore very little similarity to one another.

When I told her I wasn't interested in anything more, she went crying to Daddy, telling him how I'd broken her heart. I fully expected to be traded within the week, but lucky for me, all I got was a rap on the knuckles for being a naughty boy.

I guess Patrick O'Mara didn't want to cut off his nose to spite his face just because his little girl had gotten involved with the wrong member of his team.

That was almost six years ago, and it should have served as a total wake up call for me.

"My advice, Lennox? Leave well alone. Go find some other woman who's got no connection to the team. You want to become the new Cade Lennox? Then you're gonna have to change your ways, by which I mean don't date the team's social media manager."

I throw my hands in the air. "Okay. I won't ask her out. I'll become a monk. Happy?"

"It's not a matter of me being happy or not. You came here to turn over a new leaf. So, turn over that leaf."

I think of Clara's worried look as she rushed off after that guy Joel accidentally livestreamed our dance. She clearly thought she was in trouble. "She might have lost her job anyway."

"What makes you say that?"

"Did you see the video of us dancing on the ice?"

"That was *dancing*?" he says, and I throw my towel at him.

"She was meant to be just filming it but the guy who took over from her livestreamed it. She didn't look happy when she left."

"I guess we'll find out tomorrow at practice. Coach told us someone was coming to film."

"I guess we will."

There's a knock at the door.

"That'll be another delivery," I say as I pad across the room. "The Player Assimilation Liaison that the team gave me to help me settle in ordered a whole bunch of stuff for me. I've had more deliveries here in the past couple days than I did in a month in Manhattan." I make my way down the hallway and pull the door open, expecting a delivery guy in a uniform.

What I get makes me feel like someone shook up a soda can inside me and popped the lid.

"Well, if it's not the Triple Threat," I say as my gaze sweeps over the very woman I've just been told not to get anywhere near. Which makes her even more attractive, if I'm honest.

The lure of the forbidden.

I am *so* here for it.

Just like when we did our TikTok dance, Clara's in a navy pencil skirt and a pair of heels, this time with a long, pale blue winter coat over a white shirt, her blonde hair tied up in a modest bun at the nape of her neck. She looks like a hot librarian, only she's a hot social media manager.

At least I hope she still has the job.

She freezes for a moment before she regains her composure. "I'm sorry, did you say 'triple threat'?"

"That's what I'm calling you." I begin to count them off on my fingers. "Mom, social media manager, and, if you don't mind me saying, all 'round babe." I pause, hoping I haven't overstepped the mark. She doesn't want to like it, but the glint in her eyes says otherwise.

"You *are* still our social media manager, right?"

"I am."

"So, the livestream wasn't an issue?"

"It turns out my boss wasn't at all worried about me being on the video because it got so many likes, comments, and reposts. In fact, she wants more content with me with…well, with you."

"Me?"

"She thought we had 'chemistry,'" she replies, as though saying the word is physically painful for her.

"Chemistry. Yup, I've heard of that," I tease.

She shifts her weight. "The comments reflected that perspective." She sounds all formal and librarian-y.

Totally on-brand for her.

"Did they now?" I'm playing dumb when the fact of the matter is I watched the video more than once, and I read some of the comments. A lot of them focused on how romantic it was when I looked at her when she landed in my arms (from a chick), right through to how this isn't a freaking romcom movie, and where's the freaking hockey? (from a guy).

At the risk of agreeing with @GoalieGirl23, her landing in my arms like that did look pretty freaking romantic.

And it felt pretty freaking romantic, too.

"So, Ms. Reynolds can see what I can see, huh?" I say, but all she does is tighten her lips. "Hey, do you wanna come in? It's cold out here."

Her eyes skim over me and she tightens her lips. "That's because you spend most of your life shirtless, it would seem. You know it's fall, right?"

I look down at the now goose flesh of my chest as though just realizing my current state of shirtless-ness. "I guess you're just lucky you caught me, Triple. Come in." I stand back for her to walk inside and close the door over behind her.

"So that nickname is a thing now? What's wrong with 'Clara'?"

"Not one thing," I say, enjoying the way my comment makes her squirm.

How's the turning over of a new leaf coming along, Cade? I can almost hear Jamie's voice in my head.

I gesture behind me with my thumb. "I can go throw on a shirt."

"It's fine," she says stiffly, pulling her lips into a smile that tells me it's anything but. "I thought your Player Assimilation Liaison the Ice Breakers gave you to settle you in would be here. I was told you were at the gym."

So she checked to see I wouldn't be home before she dropped by. Perhaps she thought it would be easier not to see me, what with all this chemistry between us.

Yup, she feels it, too.

"My gym is here at the house," I explain. "And Damian's done for the day, so you've got me. I was just working out in my gym with Hayes and Crane, but we're almost done."

"Which explains why you look like," she waves her hand over me, "that."

I can't help but smile at how uncomfortable my naked torso is making her. Her eyes flick to mine and she raises her brows as though I've been a naughty kid. I bet she uses that look on her own kids all the time.

"It's nice to see you again," I say.

"Thank you," she replies, and I wonder if she thinks it's nice to see me again, too. "Actually, I'm a little flustered today. I just found out that our town is in jeopardy. There's been an emergency town meeting and everything." Her face is stricken, and concern leaps in my chest.

"Threat? What do you mean?"

"Apparently, some heir no one knew about is claiming our town and all the land around it, and he wants to redevelop it."

"Wait, *what*?"

She shakes her head, her features taut with tension. "Some guy called Alexander MacDonald. Everyone is saying he'll ruin Maple Falls, putting in all the big city stores and the like. People are freaking out."

"I bet they are."

"We've been told that he's instructed his lawyers to move

ahead, and everyone is riled up, holding our proverbial pitch-forks following an emergency town meeting a bunch of the townsfolk attended a couple days ago. We're not taking this lying down. We're going to fight it by raising money to save our town."

Her firm tone and commitment is impressive, her pretty face flushed with passion. It only makes her all the more attractive.

"What will that mean for the team, I wonder?" I say to myself more than anything.

"It could mean the team has to move to another town. Spokane or Seattle. Somewhere else within the state. That's what people are saying."

"I'll help in whatever way I can. Just say the word," I say without a second thought. I might not have been here all that long, but I've made this town my new home for the season. The last thing I want is for it to lose its small-town charm and turn into one of those bland places with zero appeal. And if the Ice Breakers have to move to another town, not only will that affect me, but it'll mean Clara would have to move, too. Either that or lose her job.

"Really?"

"Of course. This town matters to me."

Her features relax a notch. "Thank you," she breathes. "I've got some ideas."

"I bet you have, Triple." I give her a smile and enjoy the way the pink of her cheeks deepens.

"Lennox? Who is it?" Jamie's voice says behind me.

"It's Triple Threat," I call out, not pulling my eyes from hers, because I think Clara Johnson might have the most beautiful eyes I've ever seen. Big and blue and judging me. Really, it would be a crime not to look at them as much as humanly possible.

She rolls those beautiful eyes at the mention of her nickname.

"Who?" Jamie appears beside me "Oh, hey, Clara. Good to see you again," he says.

"It's good to see you again, too, Mr. Hayes," she replies.

"It's Jamie. Or Captain, if you're so inclined."

She scrunches up her nose. "I think I'll go with Jamie."

"Clara was just telling me about how Maple Falls is under threat from some heir to the town who wants to develop it," I explain.

"I heard that, too," Jamie says, which surprises me, but then he is the captain so maybe someone from Management thought he ought to know. "Is that what's in the envelope?" He gestures at what Clara's holding in her hands, which I hadn't even noticed, I was so busy being entranced by her gorgeousness.

"Actually, this is some information for the upcoming social media campaigns," she says, holding out a brown envelope for me.

"This is all the stuff you and I are going to do together?" I reply as I take it from her.

She pulls her lips into a line. "There are some general ones for volunteers, as well as the ones Veronica and I worked on this week for just you and me."

"Well, it's super nice of you to deliver it personally," I say.

"Oh, I live nearby. It's no bother."

"You live on my street?"

She gives a reluctant nod, and I bet she hadn't planned on sharing that particular piece of information with me.

"Which direction? East or west?"

"I live at the old end," she says, and I know it's a comment about the difference in our financial status more than anything geographical. According to the realtor, the house I'm renting is one of a few new, larger places that have sprung up since the town's fortunes changed following the first Ice Breaker team.

"I'll be sure to swing by for coffee sometime," I say, and she shifts her weight, looking embarrassed.

Oh, yeah. She's definitely feeling this thing between us.

I couldn't stop my smile from busting out if I wanted to. And I don't want to. Clara Johnson is one hundred percent my kind of woman. She's smart and ambitious and sexy as all get out. Who am I to fight destiny?

She ignores my suggestion. "Have a look over the ideas and let me know which activities you would like to be a part of. The same goes for you, Jamie. There's an envelope being delivered to your place, with info on a bunch of initiatives, too."

"Thanks," Jamie replies.

"All of them," I say without even opening the envelope.

She pulls her brows together. "Excuse me?"

"Sign me up for all of them," I repeat.

"But you don't even know what they involve," she protests.

I shrug. "The dancing on the ice was fun and I'm happy to do whatever the team needs me to do."

"You are *such* a team player, Lennox," Jamie says, slapping me on the bare shoulder.

"That I am, Captain," I reply, ignoring his sarcasm.

"Even the one in which you showcase a non-hockey talent?" Clara asks with a look that tells me she doesn't think I have a talent outside of hockey—or possibly outside of parading around bare-chested.

"Bring it on," I say, my smile not wavering.

"I look forward to that," she replies tightly.

I lift my lips into a grin. "I promise you, you won't be disappointed."

"Oh, good grief," Jamie says with a shake of his head.

But I don't care. Standing here, talking to this gorgeous woman, I could flirt my butt off all day long, and I know she'll do her best to bat each and every comment away.

It's like a game.

A fun, sexy game.

A game I intend to win, because I've turned that new leaf and have become a new man—a man who wants just one woman.

And she's standing right in front of me.

Who knows? Clara Johnson might just turn out to be my Hallmark movie happily ever after.

CHAPTER 7
CLARA

I LEAN BACK against the seat of my car in the parking lot outside the arena, mid conversation, waiting for the rain that's teeming outside in the dim early morning light to let up before I make my way into the office.

CHRONICWARRIOR88:

Tell me more about this new job of yours.

ME:

I thought we agreed not to share specifics?

CHRONICWARRIOR88:

> You're right. You don't need to give me details. I just want to know how you spend your days so I can picture you.

I smile at my phone. Chatting with Warrior has been the highlight of my day for months now and I love the way he shows concern for me, no matter whether it's to do with the kids or something going on in the town or, more recently, my new job. He's so different from the guys I meet who love to talk about themselves the whole time, telling me how awesome they are at whatever it is they're bragging about—and in a small town like Maple Falls, it's either hunting or fishing or hiking, or a combination of all three.

It's not like that with Warrior. He's not once mentioned hunting or how big a fish he can catch when he's out with his buddies, or even how far he can hike.

All things guys seem to think we women are looking for in a relationship.

Instead, he's nothing but sweet and thoughtful and the best listener I know.

ME:

> Since you asked, I spend my days getting content for social media, working out marketing strategies with my boss, and then posting a bunch of stuff and holding my breath, hoping it'll hit with the fans.

CHRONICWARRIOR88:

> I bet you get a bunch of likes and comments, just like you do with your @CFSMomLife

My mind instantly turns to the huge number of likes and comments the accidental livestream involving me falling into Cade Lennox's arms garnered. Not only were there many, almost too many to count, but from what I read, most of them weren't about hockey or even dancing.

They were about me and Cade.

I refocus on my conversation.

ME:

Are you charming me again?

CHRONICWARRIOR88:

You tell me.

He adds a heart emoji, and warmth spreads through my chest.

ME:

I couldn't possibly say.

CHRONICWARRIOR88:

I'm going to take that as a yes and keep on charming you.

ME:

Ready when you are. To be charmed, that is.

CHRONICWARRIOR88:

Talk about putting a guy on the spot. I'm out of touch. I don't go around charming women all that much these days.

ME:

I bet you do and you're just being modest. I bet you have them lining up.

CHRONICWARRIOR88:

Is it conceited of me to admit that I used to before I got sick?

ME:

Honesty is always the best policy.

CHRONICWARRIOR88:

> I couldn't agree more. So yeah, I wasn't short on female interest, but these days, you're the only woman I'm interested in charming.

A smile busts across my face.

ME:

> See? Totally charming.

CHRONICWARRIOR88:

> I'm only being real, but thanks for noticing.

He adds a winking emoji, and I reply with a simple heart.

CHRONICWARRIOR88:

> I'm sorry to cut this short, but I need to head to bed. I'm super low on energy today.

ME:

> I totally get it. I've been there myself. Sleep is key in your recovery.

CHRONICWARRIOR88:

> You're so wise. I wish you were in my life for real.

I bite down on my lip, my heart doing weird things in my chest.

ME:

> I wish you were in my life for real, too.

CHRONICWARRIOR88:

> One day...

The words hang in the air between us.

ME:

> One day.

ME:

Hey, I've got to get into work now. Talk tonight?

CHRONICWARRIOR88:

Of course. Bye, beautiful

ME:

Bye

I click off my phone and let out a contented sigh. My chats with Warrior are precious. We may not have met in the flesh, but I know what I have with Warrior is as real as the day is long.

So why does guilt prick at me every time Warrior calls me beautiful? Why do I feel like I'm betraying him when my mind wanders to someone else entirely?

And that person is Cade Lennox.

Cade and his flirty comments and heated looks. Cade and his shirtless-ness with all those dang muscles of his.

My phone beeps again, and I see Bailey's name.

BAILEY:

Just catching up on your livestream. Girl, that man caught you like a romcom hero.

I press my lips together as my insides do an involuntary somersault, and against my will—and my better judgment—my thoughts drift to our last encounter. The embarrassment I felt rolls over me once again, the moment when Cade pulled his front door open and I saw him standing there in all his bare-chested glory, sweat glistening on his muscular body, that ever-present flirty grin of his in place.

He knows I find him attractive. It's as obvious as a figure skating costume on an otter.

And try as I might—and I really, really tried—it was impossible not to let my gaze drop to those impressive pecs of his, those ridiculously wide shoulders, those shapely arms. This time, unlike when he strutted into the locker room wearing just a towel and a smile, he was only three feet away.

Really, there was nowhere else to look.

Okay, not nowhere else to look exactly, but it was hard not to notice, particularly when the feeling of being held in those big, muscular arms of his was so fresh in my memory.

And he's so dang flirty! The looks he throws me, the way he called me Triple Threat, the things he says. I mean, of course I knew that about him before I even met the guy. He has a reputation. He's a flirt and a partier and a total womanizer. It's all over the media.

I couldn't *not* know it.

And the way he looks at me, all smirky and sexy, with more eye contact than an interrogation expert? It just proves the fact that his reputation is spot on.

Which is precisely why I'm never going to act on my attraction to him. He's a red flag. No, scratch that. He's a flashing red neon sign that says *Bad Idea* in 10-feet tall letters.

ME:

Talk about embarrassing. Never happening again.

BAILEY:

The fans loved it.

ME:

That's its one saving grace.

I pull up the Ice Breakers social media account and search for the livestream video, skimming the list of comments.

The GRIP he had on her waist? I need to lie down.

I don't even like hockey, but I've watched this 47 times. For the... err, skating technique.

OMG did anyone else see the way he looked at her when he caught her???

I twist my mouth and scroll on.

Me: I don't believe in love at first sight. Also me: watches this video again and again.

I let out a snort so loud it echoes off my car walls. Love at first sight? *Please.* The only thing I fell for in this video was gravity, and let me tell you, gravity has zero romantic potential. Of course it wasn't love at first sight, and not just because I'd already met Cade before this mortifying moment, which means technically it wasn't first sight at all.

And yes, I know I'm being pedantic.

Let's be real here. I sure as heck wasn't gazing up at Cade Lennox with hearts in my eyes. I was looking at him with shock...and...and with gratitude. Yes, that's what it was: gratitude. Gratitude for the simple fact that he intervened between me and the cold, hard reality of butt meeting ice.

And as for Cade, he didn't look at me with anything resembling love in his eyes. More like the same look I bet he gives every woman he encounters, aka the calculating gaze of a man who's mentally filing away another conquest for his little black book.

That's not love, people. That's a predator sizing up his prey, albeit an irritatingly handsome predator who has somehow managed to get right under my skin.

I can do this. I can manage away the inconvenient attraction I have for the guy. I'll just picture him in his underwear.

No, wait. That's not helpful.

I'll picture him as a giant baby in a diaper. Ha! Yes, that's it. Cade as a giant baby in a diaper.

Done and done.

So, comment away, internet strangers. At the end of the day, Cade and I both know the truth: the only sparks flying were from his skate blades scraping against the ice as he caught me.

I scroll further and notice a comment from an account I recognize.

You've inspired so many of us! Living proof that chronic illness doesn't end your story!

Huh. I wasn't expecting *that.*

I started @CFSMomLife to document my own wellness journey, to connect with other people who understood the way chronic illness reshapes your life. Of course falling into Cade's arms on a livestream wasn't exactly planned chronic illness representation, but seeing this comment, seeing that people in my community watched this moment and felt hope? That's something I hadn't considered, and it hits me right in the heart.

I'm accidentally showing the world that chronic illness warriors can be more than their illness.

I tap out a quick reply.

@CFSMomLife:

You're right. Chronic illness may be part of our stories, but it's not the end of it. We deserve all the joy and unexpected moments life has to offer.

Even if it's falling into a known womanizer's arms on the ice. I don't type that last part, but I sure as heck think it.

I glance at the time on my phone. I'm due to meet Veronica in less than five minutes. With no let-up in the rain, I open my door, pop up an umbrella, and dash across the parking lot and into the offices, cursing as I step in a puddle, water splashing up my shin.

When I make it into the office, the whole place is abuzz with the news about Alexander MacDonald, the long-lost heir to Maple Falls and its surrounding land. Since the emergency town meeting, everyone has been throwing ideas around about how to raise the money we need to save this town we love, including the idea of a bachelor auction that I know will be crazy popular.

People will come from all over the state and beyond to get the chance to buy a date with one of the team's hunky hockey players, even if it is for just forty-five minutes. These guys are all big stars we're lucky to have on the newest team in the NHL—which, as it turns out, is the inspiration for my idea.

I knock on Veronica's door, and she calls me in to take a seat. I clasp my hands on the wooden table in front of me and begin to present my idea. "I did a bunch of research and found this idea I thought could be fun to do for both social media content as well as to raise money for the town."

"Two birds with one stone. I like where this is heading. How would it work?"

"We would get a bunch of the guys to volunteer. This wouldn't be a mandatory thing. They would wear their Ice Breaker jerseys, making them immediately identifiable as team members. People can bid on the opportunity to throw a bucket of water over them."

She shoots me an uncertain lock. "How many buckets of water will you put these poor volunteers through?"

"Just one for each of the volunteers. The highest bid wins. Otherwise, the guys might run the risk of catching hypothermia and won't be able to play, which no one wants."

"Clearly." She taps top of her ballpoint pen against her chin. "I can see how this would be fun content for the socials. It's something different. New. You're getting to know the team now, Clara. Do you think you'll be able to get volunteers?"

Immediately, my mind darts to Cade and the fact he agreed to every single one of my initiatives. "I already have one, and I'm sure I could get a bunch more. They're good guys. Friendly. Easy to get along with."

"And when would you plan on doing this?"

"I've thought about that already. It would be a fun thing to do at the farmers' market one weekend. It's the perfect place to do it. It's outside, we can set up a makeshift stage, and we could even get the mayor to MC it. It'd be a whole town event."

"I'm loving this idea, Clara. I visited that farmers' market at the weekend. It was so quaint, with lots of delicious food options and things to buy."

"My sister, Keira Roberts, runs it. I already asked her if we could run something like this. Just in case you agreed."

"Very proactive of you."

"She said she could set up a stage for the guys to stand on, provide a microphone for the mayor, donate the use of a tent for the guys to change in once they're wet, and even provide the buckets and water."

"Thank you, Clara's sister. If we do go ahead, what would we call it? Dunk a Hunk?" She grins at me.

"Soak the Skater? Oh, what about Wet and Icy?"

She mock shivers. "Or Buckets and Biceps."

We both begin to laugh.

"How about Make it Rain?" I say.

"Unless we're going to stick them in a shower…?"

"Ah, no," I reply with a laugh. I lean back in my chair as a name hits me. "Veronica, I think I've got it. Drench for Defense. It's got a double meaning: hockey defense and defending the town from redevelopment."

"Drench for Defense. It's perfect!" Veronica declares, and I can't help but feel proud of both my idea and the name I came up for it. "I can see this getting a lot of attention online. You know, I haven't lived in this town all that long, but Maple Falls has really grown on me. I love that the team could help to protect it. I suggest you start by talking with Coach Hauser. Once you've got him on board, you're halfway there."

"Will do."

"Now, have you spoken with Cade Lennox about doing some more videos with you?"

My pulse leaps at the mention of his name. "Ah, yes. He's happy to do so." My voice sounds strangled, so I clear my throat and concentrate on looking as professional as possible. Which really shouldn't be hard. I mean, it's not like we're involved or anything. He's just flirty and frequently shirtless—which is proving to be a potent combination for me.

But I've got it under control.

"That's good news. I noticed that livestream video has had over 2.3 million views. Capitalizing on that is the smart thing to do." She pauses before she adds, "But be careful with Cade, Clara. We can all see his appeal, but he has a certain reputation.

In fact, I've been told he almost got traded for carrying on with the owner's daughter at the NYC Blades six or seven years ago."

My jaw drops. "That doesn't surprise me."

He's Cade Lennox: womanizer of the year.

"Just watch yourself around him. I know we've asked you to work closely with him, but we have a non-fraternization policy for very good reasons. In fact, I would say Cade Lennox is the primary reason for it on the Ice Breakers." She smiles as though she's making a joke, but there's an undercurrent in her words that tells me to stay away from Cade in ALL CAPS.

Message received, boss, loud and clear.

"Of course, Veronica, and you can trust that I would never do anything to compromise my position here at the Ice Breakers. I love this job, and I'm determined to make a success of it."

"That's great to hear, Clara. I have total faith in you."

We spend the rest of the meeting agreeing on all the details of both Drench for Defense and my upcoming social media campaigns—both with Cade and otherwise—before I head down to the ice to catch the tail end of the team practice to get some more content.

The team is doing tough drills that could make lesser players weep. It's hard not to admire the athleticism and speed of these guys, nimbly moving around the ice and changing direction at the drop of a hat.

I begin to record the drills, noticing how the different personalities of the team members come out. The captain, Jamie Hayes, is standing at center ice, the team lining up along the boards.

"This drill simulates late-game line changes under pressure. We need to be sharper with those before our first game in a couple weeks," he says.

"You got it, Captain," Cade calls out, and I position myself to capture the team as Jamie divides them into offensive and defensive positions.

I notice Cade move into his position on the right wing.

"I want to see three passes minimum before any shot at goal.

Got it?" Jamie shouts, and the players' helmet-covered heads nod. He drops the puck and there's a burst of motion, a frenzy of athleticism and technique, Cade passing the puck to Asher, who swoops across the ice at lightning speed before he passes to Carson, who makes a successful shot at goal.

Coach Hauser blows his whistle and calls out, "Change!" and the first group of guys skate to the side and a new bunch takes over.

Having grown up in a hockey-obsessed town, with my brother-in-law Dan, joining the NHL right out of college, I've seen my fair share of games. But I've never witnessed a practice at this level, and it's mesmerizing to see the guys hone their skills, their talent and teamwork on show. Fans will lap up not only the players' skill, but the team dynamic, including Jamie's leadership that shows exactly why he has that capital "C" on his jersey.

I note Carson Crane's precision in shooting practice and capture the look on his face that screams intensity. I capture Lucian's efficiency and determination in his defensive position- ing, and Weston's prowess. Nate Simpson is constantly trying to catch the coach's attention, doing flashy moves with varying degrees of success, and I film his look of elation as Coach Hauser praises one.

I capture it every time one of the guys pats another on the back or shoulder or butt—why the butt?—to congratulate their teammate on a good shot in between drills.

I'm going to use all of this content, the ideas forming in my mind.

But as much as I'm capturing footage of each member of the team, my gaze keeps returning to Cade as he moves with prac- ticed ease on the ice. He's the embodiment of that expression "poetry in motion," his movements both fluid yet powerful, his shots confident and precise. For a player with his reputation off the ice, he sure is incredible to watch on it, and I can't help but be impressed with his sheer muscularity, speed, and strength.

By the time the team has finished, I've got enough content to keep the growing fanbase happy for weeks to come, and my next task will be to massage it into eye-catching videos and static posts.

How many of us get to record hunky men in a show of incredible athleticism for a living?

I *love* my new job.

Satisfied I have what I need, I'm about to leave when Coach Hauser tells the players the practice is done, and they begin to peel off, skating over to the exit to hit the showers. Nate Simpson is the first to reach me, and as he steps off the ice, he pulls off his helmet to reveal his blond hair stuck to his forehead, sweat drips landing on his broad shoulders.

"Hey, Claire. Did you capture that last move I pulled?" he asks with a grin.

"Which one?" I reply because I'm quickly learning that if there's one thing you can rely on with this player it's his flashy moves on the ice—that and his inability to get my name right.

"The one where I flipped the puck onto my stick while skating at full speed, then slotted it between my legs, and then over my shoulder in a perfect lacrosse-style scoop before I sniped a top-shelf shot right into the net!" he says, his face shining like polished glass as he relives the move.

I'm about to respond when Cade swoops in, clamping a gloved hand on Nate's shoulder. "That shot was risky as heck, Simpson. It could have gone all kinds of wrong."

"But it didn't. You know it was pure genius," Nate replies with a smirk.

"It was pure something," Cade replies, and he slides his grin my way that immediately sets my chest fluttering, despite how much I don't want it to.

I need to focus on Warrior. We have a real connection. He gets me and I get him. That's what matters. *Not* this annoying and inappropriate physical attraction to the wrong kind of guy.

"Well, *I* was impressed," I tell Nate pointedly. I hold my phone in the air. "All caught on video."

"Awesome! Be sure to tag me when you post," Nate says.

"I will," I promise as he takes off, leaving me alone with Cade.

Which is not a good situation to be in.

I paste on a smile and say, "Enjoy the rest of your day," before I turn to leave.

"Hey, Triple. When do you want to come over to film my talent?" he asks, and the way he says "talent" has something skittering down my spine.

Something I need to squash, STAT.

I turn back to him, Veronica's warning ringing in my ears. "Enough with the nickname, okay? This thing?" I gesture between us. "It needs to be purely professional. Got it?"

He throws me one of his knee-weakening smiles. "I am being totally professional, and besides, I can't help it that you're a triple threat."

This man is infuriating.

And hot. Definitely hot.

Dang it!

"How about we film your talent here at the rink? I've got a bunch of the team who've volunteered to showcase theirs, too. Clément recites poetry, Carson plays the guitar, Asher dances, as you know. I figure I could capture all of you in the space of an afternoon. Here. Together."

Subtext: not alone with just you and your flirty ways and risky hotness.

He looks around as though searching for something. "I'd love to, but I can't do it here, Triple."

"Why not?"

"There's no piano."

The thought of this huge, burly guy scrunched over a piano with his big fingers jabbing at the keys is akin to an elephant on ice skates: totally incongruous.

"You play piano?"

He pulls off his gloves and waggles his fingers in front of me as though this is proof of his piano-playing prowess. Which of course it isn't. It simply proves he's got big fingers.

I cross my arms and shoot him a look that tells him I don't believe for one second that he can actually play piano.

"I had lessons from the age of eight. I got pretty good, but I guess you'll see that when you come over to record me on my piano."

He's wearing that smirk that does things to me, so I pull my gaze from his and focus instead on the Zamboni as it begins its ice polishing job behind him.

"I'm sure we can find another piano somewhere for you to play." Somewhere in public with a lot of people around as a nice, thick buffer between Cade and the way he makes me feel.

"Sure," he replies, and I relax a notch. But then he leans a little closer to me and I catch his scent, an unmistakable tang of sweat, softened by the clean trace of whatever soap or deodorant he wore before practice. "But you see, I've got this problem," he says in a low, husky tone that makes the hairs on my neck prickle.

I swallow, my pulse rising. "What problem?"

"I don't like to play on any piano other than mine," he says.

I arch a sardonic eyebrow. "You don't like to play on any piano other than yours?"

"Yeah. My piano and I have a thing. We're exclusive. She gets jealous if I touch another piano."

Oh, the innuendo.

He straightens back up. "So, my place at say five? I'll introduce you to Bess."

"Bess?" I ask, a surprising snake of jealousy twisting my gut.

Jealousy? *Geez.*

"Bess is my piano."

"You named your piano?" I raise my hand. "Actually, don't answer that, and sorry but I have a thing then."

It's not a lie. I've been attending the Chronic Warriors Support Group at the Maple Falls Medical Center every week since I was strong enough to do so, and I'm certainly not going to give that up for Cade Lennox and his piano called Bess.

"How long is your thing?"

"An hour."

"Come after. I'll introduce you to Bess and I'll even fix you a meal."

"But—"

He breaks into a smile. "You know where I live. See you then, Triple."

As he turns and leaves, I realize I've just agreed to do exactly what I'd set out to avoid. And worse yet, it will be over dinner, making it an almost-date, which is the last thing I need with Cade Lennox, Mr. Flirty-Pants himself, with that smile of his that somehow manages to slip past the walls I've built, and makes my heart forget it's supposed to be impervious.

CHAPTER 8
CLARA

I ARRIVE at the Maple Falls Medical Center a couple minutes after six. Just as I'm about to push through the door, my phone beeps and I see a message from my ex. It used to spike my anxiety whenever his name would pop up, but these days it's just part of being a divorced couple with shared custody of a couple of children.

DWAYNE:

I'll pick the kids up Friday at 6.

No "does that suit you?" or anything. But then he wouldn't be Dwayne Campbell if he did. It's his weekend, which he gets every two weeks, and he travels up from Oregon each time, sometimes taking them for longer during the summer.

ME:

Sure. See you then.

I make a mental note to invite Bailey over that night before I slot my phone into my purse. I push through the glass door into the Medical Center to see the group members already sitting in a circle. Bernice Chen, a local doctor with multiple sclerosis who leads the group, is welcoming everyone to the session as is her weekly habit.

I know every single one of the members well. Sitting beside Bernice is rheumatoid arthritis sufferer Jason Rodriguez with his wife, Tasha, who comes faithfully each week as his support person. Those two are so cute, always holding hands and checking in with one another. Both of them are in their forties and have been together since high school.

#RelationshipGoals

Sitting beside the Rodriguezes tonight is Owen Thompson, and I slip into the spare seat beside him, flashing him a smile. He looks at me with weary eyes, and I know it's been a struggle for him to get here tonight. We both suffer from CFS, and whereas I've been mostly on top of my symptoms for well over a year now, he's in the thick of it all. I give his forearm a quick squeeze and he slides his eyes to mine with a brief smile.

"Welcome, Clara," Bernice says, and I hold my hand up in greeting and smile out at the familiar faces.

"Sorry I'm late. Work ran over and then I had to drop the kids at Keira's," I tell them.

"It's fantastic that you've got this new job working for the Ice Breakers," Jason says.

Marianne Chatfield, a single mom living with fibromyalgia, clasps her hands together and beams at me. "I think it's just wonderful, Clara. You're so clever with the internet. You must be a real asset to that new team."

The rest of the group murmurs their agreement.

"You're so kind. Thank you." I flush with pride. To many of the members, social media is a foreign land, populated solely by tech-savvy teens. I could have five followers of @CFSMomLife, and they'd think I was a runaway success.

"Are you pacing yourself? You need to pace yourself," Carmen says earnestly. "I learnt that very early on with my ankylosing spondylitis," she adds, referring to the inflammatory arthritis that primarily affects her spine.

"I'm doing my best, although it's a steep learning curve in my job right now. I'm making sure I've got my nutrition right, that I'm sleeping, and I'm trying not to let little things stress me out," I reply, and instantly my mind turns to Cade Lennox. Not that I would categorize Cade Lennox as a "little thing" exactly. More like a huge, hulking, masculine presence that skates across my mind on the regular in his oversized hockey player feet.

Without his shirt.

"Good for you, Clara," Bernice says with an encouraging smile. "You're a real success story for the group."

"It's been a difficult journey, which makes this all the sweeter." I've come a long way since I was first diagnosed in those dark early days, when the man I thought I could rely on skipped out on me and the kids, leaving me to fend for myself. If it wasn't for Keira selflessly moving back to Maple Falls to care for me, I don't know what I would have done.

Which is why I will buy her Neesha's cupcakes for the rest of my life.

"I can't wait until I can hold down a job again, but I can't imagine being able to do it right now," Owen says, his voice as thin as smoke in the morning air. "It's out of my reach."

"We hear you, Owen," Bernice says. "It's tough to see others doing the things we'd like to be able to do ourselves. The things we once could."

"Can you give us the inside track on the team?" Jason asks, his gaze crackling with interest. "We want *all* the info."

"She can't do that. She would have signed a non-disclosure agreement. Isn't that right, Clara?" says Martin Townsend, Crohn's Disease sufferer and box production business owner who has an opinion on most things.

"An NDA? Why? It's not like these new hockey players in town are anything special. They're just oversized men with too much testosterone who are freakishly good at pushing a puck around the ice and getting into fights," Marianne sniffs, her arms crossed in distaste. "They don't do a real job that requires real secrecy, like the CIA."

I press my lips together to stifle a smile as an image of the Ice Breakers in black suits and dark sunglasses springs to mind.

That could be a fun video.

"NDA, CIA. What is it with you and your acronyms?" Martin replies, but all Marianne does is hold up her hand as though she can't be dealing with him.

Those two have never gotten on, but I have a theory. They bicker so much because they're secretly into one another, but they're both too stubborn to make the first move.

"Have you signed an NDA, Clara?" Martin asks.

"I have," I admit.

Marianne's eyes have widened in triumph. "See? Told you."

Martin harrumphs as he leans back in his chair, his arms crossed.

"Shall we start the check-ins?" Bernice asks, although it's not really a question. Checking in with the members is how we start each of our sessions. "Let's start with you, Marianne. What kind of day is it today for you?"

"I was going to say green, until Martin was so rude to me. Now it's a bright, glowing red," she says, glaring at him through her glasses.

"You're being a drama queen again," Martin replies.

"No, I'm being honest. *You're* the drama queen," she rebuffs.

"Green. Nice," Bernice replies, ignoring the bickering. Or is it aggressive flirting? I should probably ask Cade about that. He's the king of flirtation, after all.

Wait. Why am I thinking about Cade Lennox again?

Bernice moves on. "Owen? What kind of day is it for you today?"

"I would say it's a yellow day because I'm managing basic things, but it's not exactly been easy for me," he replies.

Bernice moves around the room, and we get a green day from Jason and Tasha, a yellow day from Martin, a red day from Carmen, who always goes with the worst color in the traffic light system no matter what, until finally, it's my turn.

I tell everyone it's a green day for me.

"You have a lot of green days, Clara," Owen says, a note of envy in his voice. "How do you do it?"

"I'm further along my journey than you, Owen. I've learned what works for me, but it sure did take time," I reply.

"Time. Yeah," he says, a familiar tone of defeat in his voice.

"Today's topic is energy management, which is something we revisit often," Bernice says. "As we all know, it's something fundamental to many of our daily lives."

There's a murmur of agreement in the group, every single person in the room knowing exactly what it's like to have low energy reserves.

"We all know this isn't just about positive thinking, no matter what people may tell you," she continues.

"Positive thinking is for idiots," Martin sniffs.

Marianne immediately chirps, "You would say that."

These two. Every single week.

Bernice ignores their bickering once more because, really, we'd never get anything done if she didn't. "Although a positive mind frame is important, managing what limited energy reserves we have is a practical reality, which can differ every day. Owen has just pointed out that Clara is having a lot of green days, but we can't all expect to have green days all the time. Not even you, Clara."

"Oh, I know," I reply. "I'm thankful every day for where I am right now. I've had so many low energy days in which I could barely get out of bed, let alone be a mom or work a job. I'm so grateful for what I have right now."

Those were dark, dark days for me. Initially, early on in my journey, I had no clue why I suddenly couldn't get out of bed, why I felt so sapped of energy, like someone had shot lead into my chest and legs, dragging me down. It was following a virus that had felt like any other. Everyday tasks became a monumental struggle for me. Dwayne was no help. He would get angry at me for not being able to function, not being able to be the stay-at-home mom I was meant to be to our two small children. And I hated myself for it. Why couldn't I function the way normal people did, the way I used to function myself?

It wasn't until I'd been suffering for weeks before Keira came home from college for the summer and insisted I go to the doctor. She made an appointment with Bernice and drove me to it. After much testing, Bernice diagnosed me with CFS.

The very next week, Dwayne left me, leaving me with two kids under four. And taking Izzy with him as well, the woman I thought was my best friend.

No points for him as a husband *or* a father, and I lost a friend to boot.

Along with Keira's support, the ragtag Chronic Warriors Support Group has been a lifeline for me, and I will be forever grateful for Bernice and the rest of the gang.

"Let's start with knowing our baselines. What's a realistic energy level for you on an average day? Who would like to begin?" Bernice asks and immediately both Marianne and Martin's hands fly into the air. "Martin, we started with you last week, so let's make it Marianne's turn today."

Martin's hand instantly drops to his lap as his features twist with annoyance.

"Well, as you all know I've been managing my fibromyalgia for over four years now, so I have a pretty good idea of what's normal for me," Marianne begins when the door to the Medical Center suddenly swings open and we all turn in surprise to see who's interrupting.

It's two tall men, their respective bulks filling the doorway, smiling as though they've just arrived at a party rather than a support group.

Everyone gawks at them and murmurs about who they are rolling through the room.

Me? I blink at the familiar figures. Not one but two Ice Breakers have crashed our little get together. And one of them is none other than Cade Lennox.

He and Asher Tremblay are clearly lost, looking for...I don't know what. But it sure as heck isn't this support group.

Cade's eyes roam the room until they land on mine, and he raises his brows in greeting, as though he didn't expect to see me here.

I pull my lips into a line and look away.

What the heck is he doing here? And did he really not expect to see me? Sure, I didn't tell him my plans tonight were to come to this support group, but did he know that I was here and decided it'd be a great idea to come along?

The nerve of the guy!

"Gentlemen," Bernice says, her brows springing up in surprise. "Are you here for the Chronic Warriors Support Group?"

"Yes, we are, ma'am," Cade replies, but at least this time he's "ma'aming" a middle-aged woman and not me.

But wait. He said he's here for the group?

"Hey, Clara!" Asher exclaims. "Clara's here," he adds to Cade.

"Yeah, I see her," Cade says, his gaze landing on me once more.

"Hi, guys," I say weakly.

"Clara?" Bernice questions.

"This is Asher Tremblay and Cade Lennox," I say, and people murmur their greetings.

"Welcome, Asher and Cade. Pull up a chair and join us. Everyone, let's scoot back to make room," Bernice says, gesturing with her hands.

We do as we're told, sharing confused looks with one another as we do. No one knows why a couple of pro hockey players have turned up here tonight, although a bunch of the group look pretty excited about it.

Of course Cade places a chair between me and Owen, forcing me to make room for him while flashing me that confident smile of his. "Okay if I sit here, Clara?"

At least he didn't call me Triple Threat in front of everyone. I wouldn't want to have to explain that.

"I guess I can't stop you," I sniff.

"You sure know how to make a guy feel special," he replies, smirking like this is some kind of fun joke. He sits down and the chair immediately creaks with his bulk, and an image of it snapping under the pressure and him landing on his butt, makes me smile.

I glance across at Asher, who's also on a chair that's too small for him, as well. The two of them look like a couple of giants sitting on toddler stools.

As people chat, I lean a little closer to Cade and immediately regret it when I catch his aroma, the same aroma from the arena, *sans* sweat.

Why does Cade Lennox have to smell so dang good on top of his good looks, flirtatiousness, and charm? It's not fair. A guy with that multi-layered attractiveness should not be allowed to roam loose in the world. He's a danger to all womankind.

Particularly *this* woman.

"What are you doing here?" I hiss under my breath.

"I could ask the same," he replies without answering my question.

I lift my chin. "This is *my* support group. I come here every single week." I challenge him with my gaze. "And don't think I didn't notice you didn't answer my question."

His brows climb to meet his hairline. "*Your* support group? Do you run this thing?"

I'm working out how to reply when Bernice welcomes the two new, unexpected members to tonight's session. "Tell us why you're here, gentlemen," she says with an encouraging smile.

"Do you wanna go first?" Cade asks Asher, which doesn't surprise me in the least. I for one know that he's only here because somehow, he found out that I attend these sessions. All it does is give him another environment in which to flirt with me and make me even more uncomfortable around him.

This guy is seriously beginning to push my buttons.

Now, if the rest of me could quit doing backflips whenever he's around, everyone could get on with what they're meant to be doing, rather than feeling certain things that shouldn't be felt.

Asher clears his throat, his eyes flicking around the room. "I was talking with Cade here the other day and he suggested I try this out. I've not been to one of these things before."

"Would you like to share why, if you're comfortable doing so, Asher?" Bernice asks. "We're an open group, but we keep whatever we share within the group at all times. I can assure you of that."

Asher nods, but his lips remain firmly shut.

Unlike Cade's lips which would benefit from some duct tape right about now.

"Kinda like what happens in Vegas, stays in Vegas?" Cade asks with a grin, and I notice all the women in the room smile back at him as though what he said was utterly fascinating. Which of course it wasn't. It was just an overused cliché and totally inappropriate for a support group.

"I love Vegas," Marianne simpers. "Have you spent a lot of time there, Cade?"

Martin harrumphs, leaning back in his chair and crossing his arms again.

Cade shrugs. "A few times, I guess. My last team, the New York City Blades, played there a bit, of course. We beat the Knights there in the playoffs last season."

"The playoffs? You must have been so proud," Carmen says.

Oh, good grief.

"It's a good feeling whenever you beat another team. Right, Asher?" Cade says.

"Yeah, it's the best," Asher agrees.

"I'm not sure Vegas or hockey is exactly a Chronic Warriors topic," I protest, hoping to get this session back on track. But it falls on deaf ears.

"Do you gamble, Cade?" Carmen asks, her voice equally simpering. "Cade. That's a nice name. Is it short for anything?"

"Nah, just Cade, and I'm not much of a gambler. Me? I like the shows. The Cirque du Soleil ones are pretty good. Oh, and I saw Garth Brooks there not that long ago. Even got to meet the guy. He was awesome. I'm a big fan," he replies.

"I love Garth Brooks, too," Tasha says and receives a sharp look from her husband. "What? It's true, sweetheart."

I'm about to open my mouth in an attempt to get us back on track—and away from this embarrassing and entirely unnecessary fangirling over hockey players—when Bernice does the job for me.

"Shall we get back on topic?" she asks. "Asher, feel free to share why you're here tonight, if you so wish. If not, we'll move on."

Asher's features tighten, and I feel for the guy. He's clearly anxious, and I wonder whether he's here for a genuine reason—or just along for the ride with Mr. Vegas.

"I'm happy to share," Asher begins. "I know you all probably think we hockey players are pretty invincible," he begins, his hands clasped tight in his lap. "We're big and strong and athletic. Don't get me wrong, I'm healthy. You know, I don't have a disease exactly."

"Illness can take many forms, Asher. In this room right now

we have people with differing diagnoses, but we all share a common journey."

"I...I guess I do have a thing," he says, glancing at Cade, who shoots him an encouraging look.

"You got this, man," Cade says.

Asher continues, "I've got these rituals, you know? Things I've got to do to keep sane."

"Like what?" Martin asks, leaning his elbows on his knees.

"The tape on my stick needs to be in a certain symmetrical pattern, and if I don't get it looking exactly the way I like, I redo it until it overlaps precisely half an inch each time over the twenty-four wraps. Or like when I get my game gear on, I need to do it in the same order every time. No changes."

"What happens if you don't do these things?" Carmen asks, enraptured.

Asher shakes his head, his lips pulled into a line. "I've never risked it." He returns his gaze to his clasped hands in his lap.

"You're doing good," Cade encourages once more.

Asher's chest rises and falls before he looks back up at us. "The thing is I was diagnosed with OCD a while back. Obsessive Compulsive Disorder. With the move across country to this new town and new team, I guess it's flared back up, and I've been trying to get on top of it. Cade noticed and we got to talking. Then he found this group and suggested I come along."

Cade beams at him like a proud father. Which is so weird, not to mention utterly unsettling. I had this guy pegged as a total lightweight who loved to flirt. A playboy with as much depth as a puddle after a summer shower.

Not someone who encourages a teammate to attend a support group to help him with his OCD.

"Good for you," Bernice says, and there's a general agreement within the group. "Quite a few top athletes have OCD, Asher. Royce White, Simone Biles, David Beckham, Rafael Nadal, to name a few."

"See? That's what *I* said," Cade adds.

"Lennox said you guys would get it." Asher's features relax, and I slide my eyes to Cade to see him watching his teammate with a mixture of pride and kindness in his eyes.

Huh.

"We do get it, and we're here for you. Isn't that right, everyone?" Bernice says, and we all echo, "Right."

Asher's features relax, transforming him back to the guy I know once more, the guy who led his teammates in the TikTok dance with such certainty, such confidence. Who knew this other side of him lurked beneath, a side that needs routines and orderliness, without which, anxiety takes hold.

"That's great to hear," Asher says. "Cade said these groups are awesome and have really helped him."

Wait, what?

I swivel around to gawk at Cade. Not only is he perceptive and supportive of Asher, but he also attends support groups?

Why?

Cade clears his throat. "I find it super useful to get tips on things like self-care and energy management for my mom. She has lupus," Cade explains.

Cade's mom has lupus? And he attends support meetings so he can help her and learn how to cope?

My jaw has officially hit the floor.

"And what about you, Cade?" Bernice asks, her voice soft. "What do you find useful in groups like ours?"

She's a smart one, that Bernice. Always able to read the subtext, to follow the trail left unwittingly behind, and this is one trail I'm fascinated to hear.

Cade pauses for a beat. "I guess it does a bunch of stuff for me. It reminds me that my mom isn't alone in her suffering, which is comforting, you know? I guess there's something in it for me, too, in that I feel...less alone, I guess."

I still. This new side to him doesn't fit with everything I know about this man and his flirty, carefree, womanizing ways. Could a guy who cares that deeply for his mom, goes out of his way to learn strategies to help her, shows kindness and understanding toward a teammate, also be a total party boy who doesn't appear to think deeply about *anything*?

I watch him as he continues to talk, my mind scrambling to make sense of these two incongruous versions of him. He speaks with love in his voice about his mom, how hard he found it to move across the country away from her, how he hopes to bring her here if he signs with the team for another season.

As I listen, the only conclusion I can draw is that perhaps I've misjudged him.

And if I have misjudged him and his depth is less like a puddle and more like an ocean, could I be in some serious trouble here?

His gaze sweeps to mine and my breath catches, the sincerity in his eyes plain to see. Cade Lennox has depths I never suspected, and I may very well be in more trouble than I ever imagined.

CHAPTER 9
CADE

I'VE LIT the fire and flicked on a few of the lamps in the living room when Clara's car pulls into my driveway for our agreed time to film my "player talent."

I'd noticed Asher's rituals before practice, the way he always has to tap things a certain time, the way he does things in a certain order. I had a teammate in college who was exactly the same, and he'd told me that big life changes always made his symptoms that much worse.

I figured the amount of change Asher had been through in leaving his last team and moving to Maple Falls had probably gotten into his head. And you know what? Although I didn't plan it, in going to the support group tonight—heck, I didn't even *know* Clara had a chronic condition, let alone the fact she attends a weekly support group here in town—it had a certain serendipity to it.

Not that I'd ever tell the guys that. The idea of a romantic serendipity is w*aaaay* too rom-com-y.

Plus there's the fact that Clara and I aren't romantically involved.

Not yet anyway.

And yeah, I know that sounds pretty cocky. But I've seen the way she looks at me, the way her cheeks flush when I smile and flirt, the way the sight of my bare chest makes her go all fidgety and weird. She likes me. She's attracted to me.

She just won't admit it.

There's a knock at the door, and I do a quick check that the room is tidy, shoving a pair of sneakers I threw off last night under one of the sofas with my foot. Although the style of the house is completely different from my condo in Manhattan, the place came furnished with its quaint, small-town vibe, which is fitting, what with this house being in a small town and all.

Totally on brand, as my agent would say.

If I end up signing for another season or more, I'll buy my own place and bring the rest of my stuff over from NYC.

But this will do for now.

As I pull the door open, a cold blast of air hits me, and I slide my eyes over Clara. She's still in her work clothes, totally rocking her pencil skirt and blouse, over which she's thrown the winter coat I saw her in at the arena. Her hair is captured in a low bun which, combined with the glasses she's wearing, gives her that totally hot librarian vibe.

Not that she looks like any of the librarians I've ever known.

I imagine loosening her hair so that it falls around her shoulders, and gently removing her glasses before I lean in and—

"Are we staying on the doorstep or are you going to invite

me in?" she asks as she removes her glasses and slots them in a case.

I'm forced to shake myself out of my sexy librarian daydream. As fun as it was.

"Yeah. Sorry. Come on in." I stand back for her, and she breezes past me, her pretty, floral scent following her. "Can I take your coat?"

She shrugs it off and passes it to me.

"I didn't know you wore glasses."

"Just for driving and going to the movies. I see you've chosen to wear a shirt this time. That's a good start."

"I can take it off if you prefer?" I tease, fingering the bottom of my hoodie, and immediately she shakes her head, holding her hands up in the *stop* sign.

"Thanks, but I'm good."

"The offer is always there, Triple. Just say the word."

I watch as her cheeks grow pink. Man, I love it when they do that. It brings out the blue in her eyes, making them sparkle all the more. Not to mention the fact it reconfirms my hunch that she's into me.

Not that she'd ever admit to that. Clara Johnson is proving to be one hard nut to crack.

I hang her coat on the rack and then lead her to the living room. She looks around at the tan leather sofas and the fireplace with its now roaring fire. The place is cozy, inviting, and warm. The temperature is still pretty mild here in Maple Falls during the day, but when it drops at night, it sure is good to get cozy by the fire.

"That didn't used to be there," she says as she points at the TV above the fireplace.

"You've been here before?"

"I grew up in Maple Falls. I've been to pretty much every house in town, even this one. It's owned by the O'Connors. They invited everyone in the neighborhood over for coffee when they moved in."

"Bill and Jen. That's right. Nice people."

She nods, her lips pulled into a line. "Is that Bess?" she asks as she moves across to my baby grand. Bess has pride of place near the french doors that open onto the generous yard, and I love to sit there and play early in the mornings when I don't have practice, looking out the windows at the greenery.

"Yup, this is my baby." I run a hand across Bess's varnished wood. "A masterpiece in refinement and craftsmanship. She was handcrafted in Austria."

"She?" she asks with a laugh. "Should I be impressed by that?"

"Oh, yeah. You should be. Bess is the best you can get."

"A bosen-what? How do you pronounce that?" she asks, reading the gold lettering above the keys, and I smile at her pronunciation.

"Bösendorfer," I say. "That's the make. These pianos are known for their warm, rounded tone. Very resonant."

She looks at me as though I'm speaking a foreign language. Either that or she's surprised to hear such words fall from my mouth.

"I'll take your word on that. We've got one of those upright pianos I bought from a secondhand place when Hannah began learning to play. It's plain wood and sounds kinda clunky. This piano is definitely next level." She lightly touches the keys.

"May I?" I ask.

"May you what?"

Instead of telling her, I slide my hand over hers and depress her thumb, then middle finger, and then her pinkie, and a chord sounds out. "Hear that? That's the resonance." Her hand is small beneath mine, the touch of her skin as soft as I'd thought it would be.

She lifts her lips in a nervous smile, and I know I've overstepped the mark.

I pull my hand away. "I shouldn't have done that. It was instinct."

"It's fine. Really," she replies, clasping her hands together. "When do I get to hear you play?"

"All good things take time, you know, Triple," I reply, slipping easily back into playful default mode. "But first, let's eat. I'm starving. You?"

"I can have something quick. I need to go pick up the kids after filming."

"Where is my comic book buddy tonight?"

"He and his sister are with their aunt and uncle. They'll be spoiling them rotten."

"Of course they will. That's their job."

"You know about these things?"

"Got my uncle badge, and proud of it. My sister, Tori, and her husband have twins. Oliver and Olivia. I see them when I can."

"Where are they?"

"Back in the New Jersey town I grew up in. They live a couple streets over from my mom."

By now we've reached the kitchen, where she takes a seat on one of the stools, leaning her elbows on the kitchen counter.

I pull a packet from the refrigerator. "I've got some fresh pasta. I could make a sauce."

"You cook?"

I waggle my brows at her suggestively. "I'm a man of many talents, Triple."

She shakes her head at me, but she's smiling, not frowning.

"What?" I say.

"You just don't quit, do you?" There's a lightness to her voice that wasn't there before.

"Not when it comes to beautiful social media managers for the Ice Breakers," I tease. "Do you want a soda? I'd offer you wine, but I don't drink during preseason or the season."

"A soda's great."

I pull a couple of cans from the refrigerator, and we both crack them open.

"Here's to Chronic Warriors," I say.

"To the Chronic Warriors," she echoes, and we clink cans before we both take a sip. Placing her can on the counter, she says, "Tell me about your mom. You said she has lupus. That must be tough."

I get to work on making the pasta sauce, chopping up some pancetta. "It's not easy for her. It took seven years before she was diagnosed and her symptoms kept getting dismissed by multiple doctors, telling her she just needed to reduce stress, whatever that means. That was going on when I was a senior in high school and right through college. She finally got diagnosed after she had a severe flare up that even the stupid doctors couldn't ignore."

"Bernice talks about how long it can take to get a diagnosis for a bunch of autoimmune disorders. It can be years and years."

"Yup, that's what happened with my mom. She was diagnosed just before I got signed with the Blades. I chose them because it was close to her in New Jersey. It meant I could check in with her or get to her fast if she needed me."

The guilt in leaving her on the other side of the country to join the Ice Breakers twists in my belly. I've never lived this far away from my mom. Although she's doing better now and she has my sister nearby, there's a part of me that still thinks I should never have left, even though she's excited at the chance to move here if things pan out.

She's the reason I didn't sign for more than one season. If Tori is finding it too much, if my mom has a serious setback, I can get back there.

"You're a long way from her here in Washington state," Clara says, as though reading my mind.

"She insisted I go. She's so concerned with not being a burden, sometimes it drives me crazy, you know? I try to get her the best doctors, the best care, but sometimes it's hard to get her to take it. She is one stubborn woman."

Her eyes flash to mine. "A little like her son?"

"What makes you say that?"

"I've seen you at practice. You really push yourself in those drills. You refuse to give up."

"Had to. Coach's instructions."

She smiles. "For what it's worth, Cade, it sounds to me as though you're a great son. You wouldn't have come to the support group tonight if you weren't."

"I don't know," I say, that guilt still heavy in my stomach. "If Tori wasn't around, I wouldn't be here."

"You've got to live your life, too."

"I guess."

Her phone rings in her purse, and she climbs down from the stool and walks into the living room to answer it as I busy myself making a carbonara sauce out of the pancetta, eggs, thickened cream, and parmesan, the ingredients lined up on the counter in a way even Asher would approve of.

I'm about to place the fresh fettuccini pasta into a pot of boiling water when she returns, still holding the phone to her ear. "Everything okay?"

She holds her hand over the phone's mouthpiece. "I'm sorry, Cade, but I need to go."

Disappointment slams into me. "What? Why?"

"My sister's husband is out, and she has the kids, but she's been called into work. She runs the town's farmers' market and apparently there was some problem."

"Have her drop them off here."

Her eyes widen. "Here?"

"Why not? I can show Benny my comic collection, and I can easily make more pasta sauce if they haven't eaten."

"You want my kids here in this fancy house? Are you serious?"

"One hundred percent. Do they like fettuccini carbonara?"

She appears to think about it for a moment before she thanks me and lifts the phone to her ear once more. "Cade says the kids can come here for some pasta, so can you drop them off on the way? It's the O'Connor's house." Her sister must remark on the house because Clara replies, "You know these hockey players. They love their fancy houses."

I shrug because she's right. "We're big guys. We need big places."

"Okay. See you in ten." She hangs up and puts her phone on the counter. "What can I do to help?"

"Do you and your kids like tomatoes on your salad?"

"Sure do."

I push a board and knife over toward her and grab a couple of tomatoes from the bowl on the counter behind me. "Chop these babies right up."

She runs some water, washing the tomatoes. "Can I be honest with you?"

"That depends on whether or not you're planning on saying something nice," I tease as I stir the mixture in the pot.

She smiles. "It's nice."

"Then throw that honesty right at me, Triple."

She begins to slice the tomatoes. "You're not the guy I thought you were."

"That's because I'm like a seven-layer dip, just with more emotional depth and less guacamole."

"So what you're saying is, you pair well with chips?" she asks, and I let out a laugh.

"Sure. Let's go with that."

"I'm embarrassed to admit that I thought you were all about flirting and having fun, without any other dip layers."

"You see, that's only my top layer."

"So I'm beginning to learn."

We share a look, and my belly does a weird somersault thing I'm definitely not talking to the guys about at practice tomorrow.

"I heard a rumor," she begins.

"It's all true. I am total boyfriend material."

She laughs, shaking her head. "Are you ever serious?"

I put down my knife and look at her. "What's the rumor?"

"It was from my boss, actually. Veronica Reynolds. She told

me about how you had a thing with the New York City Blades owner's daughter and nearly got traded when it went sour."

Her words take me by surprise, but it's the truth, so I say as much.

She blinks at me in shock. "You're not going to deny it?"

"Of course not. Misty O'Mara, the owner's daughter, approached me, being very explicit about wanting what she called a 'no strings attached fling with the team's playboy.' Her words, not mine, though I'll admit, at the time, that reputation wasn't entirely undeserved. I thought we were both clear on the terms. I was young, stupid, and flattered by the attention." I pause, catching Clara's eye. "Wisdom and hockey players don't always go hand in hand."

"What happened?"

"She told me she wanted more than I was willing to give. She then went to her dad, telling him that I'd broken her heart."

"Did you? Break her heart, I mean?"

"Nah. I think Misty was just angry with me that I ended it first. She moved on pretty fast, marrying another guy on the team before the year was out. I think it was more her ego that was broken than anything."

"Wait. Misty Petrenko? Married to the Blades's defenseman, Stepan Petrenko?"

"Look at you with your hockey knowledge."

"More Instagram knowledge, if I'm honest. She's got a big following. She's beautiful."

I resume my task, stirring the sauce and adding the parmesan cheese. "You're right across social media, huh?"

"I guess. I used it with my CFS to reach out to others, and it became an important part of my healing process."

"Like the Chronic Warriors."

"Exactly. Connection with others can show us we're not alone. But then you know that already, hence your coming tonight."

I look up at her. "You know, I said you were a triple threat, but I think you're actually quadruple."

"Why?"

I count them off on my fingers. "Because not only are you a total babe, a mom, and a social media expert, but you're smart, too."

"Thanks?" she says with a laugh, and I watch for that familiar cheek flush, and when it happens I want to punch the air.

Either that or kiss her.

Man, do I want to kiss her.

But instead, we work side by side to make fettuccini carbonara as though cooking together is something we've done for an eternity, rather than just this one time.

It feels nice. Homey. A guy could get used to having a woman like Clara Johnson around.

I serve up the food, keeping some behind for her kids, and we chat about inconsequential things as we eat, and I learn more about this woman who can knock the air right out of me with just one look.

I catalogue the facts in my mind as she speaks, everything from her favorite music to the fact she was a cheerleader in high school—which creates a new image in my head to rival even the hot librarian.

Just as I insist that I clear the table, the doorbell rings and Clara springs to her feet. "That'll be Keira and the kids. Do you mind if I get it?"

"Be my guest."

I hear them before I see them, their excitement at seeing their mom and telling her about the things they've been up to filling the air. I wipe my hands on a towel and make my way around the counter to greet them.

"Hey, Benny," I say when I spot my little comic buddy. I hold out my hand for a low high five, which he takes with enthusiasm. "You worked it out yet that Zara Kazan is the true hero of *The Timekeeper Chronicles*?"

"No way! It's Max," he says vehemently, sticking to his favorite.

I smile at the pretty blonde woman and the girl, who looks a lot like her mom and her aunt. "Hey, I'm Cade," I say.

"I'm Keira Roberts, and this is Hannah," she replies, her hands on Hannah's shoulders.

"Hey guys. Great to meet you," I say, shaking Keira's hand and high fiving Hannah, who does so more cautiously than her brother.

The family resemblance is strong, each person with varying shades of blond hair, and all with those big piercing blue eyes Clara possesses.

"It's so kind of you to have not only Hannah and Benny, but Clara, too," Keira says, and I think I detect a playful tone in her voice.

"Your sister is such a handful," I tease, my gaze flashing to Clara's.

Keira's blonde and pretty, objectively speaking, and she and Clara could pass for twins at a pinch. Same hair, same delicate features, same blue eyes. But where Keira's smile is perfectly nice, Clara's smile hits me like a sucker punch to the solar plexus.

Keira's eyes brighten. "That she is. Hey, I'm sorry to drop and run, but I've gotta go," Keira says, giving her sister a kiss on the cheek.

"Thanks again, sis," Clara says.

"As long as you two had a good time, then it's all worth it," Keira replies, and Clara throws her a warning look that makes me chuckle.

"We've had a wonderful time. Right, Clara?" I say, and Keira nudges her sister, who looks totally mortified by the conversation.

And yup, that makes me laugh some more.

"See you later, munchkins," Keira says to the kids, and then she throws us a wave and leaves.

"Hey, Benny. Let me show you something," I say.

"What?" he asks.

I pad over to the wooden cabinet by the dining room and pull the doors open. Benny's eyes grow to the size of hockey pucks as he takes in my *The Timekeeper Chronicles* collection of comic books, framed posters, collectible action figures—still in their boxes—and other merch.

"You've got *everything*!" he exclaims.

"Not everything, but it's true, I've got a lot of the merch." I pick up one of the framed pictures I plan on hanging on the wall. "This is from the comic book illustrator. I met her in Vegas a few years back. She's super talented."

"Wow!" He swivels to look at Clara. "Mommy, have you seen this?"

"I'm seeing it now," she replies.

Benny bounces on the spot. "You've even got an action figure of Max Griffin. He's my favorite!"

I collect the box and pass it to him. "Take it. It's yours now."

His already huge eyes bulge. "Seriously?"

"Seriously."

"Cade, you don't need to do that," Clara interjects.

"I know I don't, but I want to," I say with a shrug, because watching Benny's ecstatic expression as he turns the toy over in his hands is better than any collectible.

"Let me at least pay you for it," she offers.

"Not happening," I say, making my way over to Clara's daughter. "Hey, Hannah, right?" I ask and she nods. "I hear you play the piano."

"You're not going to give her your piano, are you?" Clara says and I waggle my brows at her as though I just might.

"I only started lessons this year, but I hope to be as good as Leo Garabaldi by the Show Quest," she says.

"How good is Leo Garibaldi?"

"He's going to play 'Believer.'"

"The Imagine Dragons song?" I ask and she nods.

"I want to play a Taylor Swift song, but my teacher thinks I should play 'Twinkle, Twinkle, Little Star.'"

"When's this Show Quest?" I ask.

"It's the week before Thanksgiving, but I'm not sure I'll enter." Her features drop.

"Why not?" I ask.

"Hannah had a bit of a bad experience at her figure skating showcase last month. She's got a touch of stage fright now that we're working on. Right, sweetheart?" Clara says.

Hannah gives a grim nod, her little mouth pulled into a line.

I do some mental math. The week before Thanksgiving is just under two months from now. If she's only just started lessons, she's got a steep learning curve to learn a Taylor Swift song by then.

I lean my hands on my knees to reduce my 6'4" frame, getting closer to Hannah's height. It's fair to say there's still a sizable gap between us. "You know, I've got a piano. Wanna check it out?"

Hannah looks wary.

"It's a baby grand made in Austria," Clara adds. "Cade said it's top of the line. He calls it Bess. Can you believe that, sweetheart?"

Hannah twists her mouth. "Bess?"

"That's right. Come on. I'll play something with you." I flash my eyes to Clara's, and she shoots me a grateful look.

"That sounds fun, sweetheart," she encourages.

"I guess," Hannah replies and together we make our way to the piano, where I pull the stool out for us both to sit down.

"What do you know how to play?"

"'Mary Had a Little Lamb,' 'Twinkle, Twinkle, Little Star,' and 'Chopsticks,' although Mommy doesn't like that one."

"It's just that you play it a lot, honey," Clara explains.

"It's because it's fun!" Hannah replies.

"I've got an idea. How about we play 'Chopsticks' together and show Mommy just how good it can be?" I suggest.

Benny laughs from his position by the cabinet, the action figure in his hands. "She's not your mommy!"

"You've got a point there, Benny," I say, my eyes flashing to Clara's. Her face is lit up in a smile, and my belly does that somersault thing again. "Right, 'Chopsticks.' You know this part, right?" I play the tune and Hannah nods. "All right. You play that and I'll add to it. Ready, maestro?"

"Ready," Hannah says and immediately begins to play the tune. Once she's completed one iteration, I add some harmony, hamming it up like I'm some professional pianist, which makes Benny laugh and Hannah crack a smile. The best bit? I notice Clara is absolutely beaming. So, I add some flourishes, really getting into it as Hannah's little tongue pokes out in concentration. Yeah, I'm definitely showing off now, but not for the usual reasons.

This isn't about impressing anyone or playing the charming hockey star. This is about being part of something real, something that has nothing to do with the ice or the team or any of the noise that usually fills my world.

It's just us. Just this moment. Clara beaming from the couch as she watches us, Benny giggling at my theatrical flourishes, Hannah proud of holding her own. It's simple and it's perfect and it's everything I know I've been missing.

This is what a family feels like, and with Clara, I begin to feel I could build something lasting, something solid and real.

For the first time in my adult life, I'm not thinking about the next game, the next season, or what anyone expects from me. I'm just here, in this moment, it feels like this is exactly where I'm supposed to be.

CHAPTER 10
CLARA

I SNUGGLE BACK onto the back of the sofa, Bailey sitting with her legs up on the seat opposite as we sip chamomile tea. I'm thankful that another work week is over. My energy levels have held up well to the demands of my new job so far, but I'm not taking anything for granted. This is too big of an opportunity for me to burn myself out. I need to do exactly what Bernice told us all to do at the last support group meeting and treat myself kindly, allowing myself the space to rest and recuperate.

That's not to say my job isn't going crazy well. The livestream was a runaway success, despite my concerns, and several of the videos I've posted have gone viral, garnering multiple views, likes, and re-posts. Veronica pulled me to the side this afternoon to tell me how well I'm doing and how pleased Management is with my work.

It feels good to know my work is landing the way I had hoped, and Dwayne has come to Maple Falls to see the kids for the weekend, so Bailey and I can sit and chat and I know I can sleep in tomorrow if I need to.

My phone beeps beside me and I lift it to see a message from Warrior.

CHRONICWARRIOR88:

I've been thinking about you a lot today.

I smile but notice the flush of pleasure at receiving a message from him is dimmer than usual, and I know I have one person to blame for that.

Cade Lennox. Or rather Cade Lennox with his confusing layers, showing me that he's not the person I judged him as. He's managed to eke his way through my defenses and touch my heart in a way I never saw coming.

The way he cares for his mom, concerned that he's far away from her even though he knows his sister is close by; the way he bonded not only with Benny over comic books, but with Hannah, too, playing "Chopsticks" on his piano he calls Bess; the way he wanted to help out a teammate who was struggling, bringing him to the Chronic Warriors Support Group and offering him words of support.

If it wasn't for the fact he's so dang flirty, I would never have matched the Cade I'm growing to know with his public persona, the person he leads with, aka Mr. Womanizer, partying hard every day of the week.

I'm embarrassed to admit it, but I did a deep dive on him last night after I'd put the kids to bed. Everything I read suggested he's the guy I judged him as when we first met: shallow, up for a good time, never serious about anything, with a different woman on his arm in every picture.

Not once did I read anything about his mom's lupus, or about how he signed with the Blades to be near her. It's as though he has a certain image he projects that tells only part of the story, leaving out the parts that matter the most.

I've seen him a couple of times at the arena since that evening at his place when I went to film him playing the piano and instead ended up having dinner with him and seeing the way he was so natural with my kids. Truth be told, I've been avoiding him—not an easy thing to do when my job is literally to capture footage of him and his teammates for our socials.

Despite the fact she doesn't have a full picture of him, Veronica's warning about Cade rings loud and clear in my ears. It's taken me so long to get back on my feet since I was diagnosed and Dwayne left me. The last thing I want to do is throw that all away because I've got growing feelings for a man who could probably have any woman he wants, feelings that have begun to go beyond just physical attraction.

Why would he go for a single mom in her early thirties with barely two pennies to rub together?

Then I think of the way he looks at me with such softness in his eyes, the way he relates so effortlessly to my kids, the way he seems like such a genuine guy with a good heart, and I know he has feelings for me.

But I can't go there with him.

I need to focus on Warrior. Straightforward, uncomplicated Warrior, the man who cares for me, the man I've connected with through our shared illness.

"Who's that?" Bailey asks.

"Warrior."

She lets out a whistle. "Mystery Man himself, huh? How are you feeling about him?"

"I don't know. I mean, I was certain before—"

"Before someone made your heart pump harder than it's pumped before?"

I twist my mouth, my mind instantly turning to Cade.

"Girl, you're stuck between a rock and a hard place. Mystery Man being the rock, and Cade Lennox being the hard place."

I shake my head. "Thanks for the imagery."

"Okay. Answer me this. Who makes your heart beat the fastest? Mystery Man or the Ice Breakers' star winger?"

I press my lips together. I don't even have to think to know the answer. The star winger wins every time.

Bailey arches her brows at me. "You know, don't you?"

I let out of breath. "I want it to be Warrior."

"But it's Cade," she says and I nod. "You're allowed to like him, you know. Just because you've had one epically bad relationship doesn't mean you're banned from having butterflies forever."

"I know."

"Mystery Man is sweet, and I know you two have some history. But he's an idea, Clara. Cade is real. And *you* are real. You deserve to feel things, even if they're complicated, swoony things."

"But he's got his reputation."

"You said you've seen him with your kids. He gave your son a collectible action figure and played piano with Hannah. That's not a fling guy move."

I let out a surprised laugh. "Sure, he's not the guy I thought he was, but I've still got a non-fraternization clause in my contract."

"Can't you just like him from a distance? Appreciate those abs you say he shows off to you at every turn?"

"They are some pretty fine abs," I agree.

"You're not breaking rules just because your hormones are having a little revival post Dwayne the Rat."

"I guess not."

She throws her gaze over me. "But you do want to act on it. Don't you, Clara?"

Worry grasps at my chest. There are too many reasons not to get involved with Cade, the non-fraternization clause in my contract being just one of them. But then I think of the look in his eyes as he gazes at me and the worry loosens. He's not the man I thought he was. He's so much more, and it's impossible not to want to have that kind of man in my life.

"Girl, you're in deep," Bailey says, shaking her head.

I let out a sigh. "What would you do if you were me?"

"I guess I would work out if he was worth the risk."

An hour later, Bailey heads home and I pick up my phone to respond to Warrior's message.

> ME:
>
> Why have you been thinking about me today?

> CHRONICWARRIOR88:
>
> Because I read that Maple Falls could be redeveloped.

> ME:
>
> We're raising money to try to stop that from happening.

> CHRONICWARRIOR88:
>
> How?

> ME:
>
> The townsfolk are being so creative and resourceful. There are a bunch of initiatives, including one I came up with myself.

> CHRONICWARRIOR88:
>
> What's your idea?

> ME:
>
> We're calling it Drench for Defense. We're going to get people to bid on a bucket of water to throw over one of the Ice Breakers. The highest bid wins and hey presto, wet hockey player.

> CHRONICWARRIOR88:
>
> That sounds chilly at this time of year.

ME:

These guys can cope.

My mind instantly leaps to the way the water clung to Cade's ripped torso that time I spoke to the team in the locker room, and a wave of guilt rolls over me. I can't think about one guy wearing nothing but a towel as I'm chatting with another online. It might not be being unfaithful exactly, but it sure lies somewhere in the territory.

ME:

How are you feeling today? How are your energy levels?

CHRONICWARRIOR88:

I am cautiously optimistic that your advice over the past couple months is helping me.

I straighten my back, sitting upright.

ME:

Seriously? That's amazing!

CHRONICWARRIOR88:

You're the one who's amazing. I'm just the lucky schmuck who found you.

I blow out of breath. Even just a couple weeks ago if Warrior had said something like that to me my heart would have expanded to twice its size.

But that was before Cade.

ME:

You're so sweet, but it's you doing the work, not me.

CHRONICWARRIOR88:

Thanks to you. Talk tomorrow?

ME:

Sure.

CHRONICWARRIOR88:

Night, beautiful

ME:

Night.

I pull off the warm blanket covering my legs and instantly feel the chill. The heating went off a good thirty minutes ago, and that's my signal to head to bed. As I'm brushing my teeth, my phone pings once more. Assuming it's Warrior again, I pick it up and am surprised to see a message from Cade. And of course my heart leaps.

CADE:

Triple, I hope it's not too late at night to message you but I had an idea while I was working out with some of the guys.

He's refusing to give that nickname up, and I admit, I'm not mad about it. Even if it isn't exactly professional. But then the other night at his place with Hannah and Benny wasn't exactly professional, either.

CADE:

Shirtless, in case you were wondering.

Of course he is. I ignore the reference in my message back to him.

ME:

For what?

CADE:

It's about Hannah.

I pull my brows together. Hannah?

My phone rings in my hand, making me jump.

I spit out the toothpaste in my mouth and give it a quick rinse. "Hi, Cade," I say as my pulse begins to return to normal. Or at least as normal as it gets around him, which isn't really normal at all.

"Did I wake you?"

"No. I was just brushing my teeth, getting ready for bed."

"I hope you're in a sexy black nightie," he says.

I chortle. I'm not going to play his flirty game, not when I have the dangerous, career-ending feelings I do for this man. "What can I help you with?"

"You know how well Hannah and I played Chopsticks together the other night on Bess?"

I soften. "You were great with her, and I appreciate it."

"Save your compliments for later, but make sure you make them, okay?"

I smile. That's *so* Cade.

"I want us to enter Show Quest."

I pull my eyebrows together in confusion. "Cade, what are you talking about?"

"Isn't it obvious? I want to enter the Show Quest competition with Hannah. That way, I can help her get over her stage fright, and together we can play one of the songs she likes by Taylor Swift, and win!"

I feel as though I've stepped into an alternate universe in which hockey pros play musical instruments with my kids for fun. "You want to enter Show Quest with Hannah?"

"Were you not listening, Triple? That's exactly what I'm telling you."

"Last time I checked, you're not a kid at Maple Falls Elementary."

"Duh."

"Did you just 'duh' me?"

"Look, I've been asking around about the rules for Show

Quest and apparently, as long as the kid is front and center as the primary performer, an adult—which in this case will be me—can give an assist. And yes, I did use a hockey term there. You're welcome."

I lean against the basin. "I'm not sure that's a great idea."

"Why not? It solves all Hannah's problems. I can help her practice, and then I can be beside her when she performs. It's a win-win."

"For Hannah?"

"For Hannah and for me."

"What exactly do you win?"

"The admiration of her mom."

I can't help but laugh. *This man!*

"So? What do you say? I can practice with Hannah in the afternoons after school."

"She's got figure skating Thursdays."

"On the afternoons except for Thursdays, then."

I chew on my lip. "Her dad will be at Show Quest, you know. I'm not sure he'll be exactly thrilled that his daughter is playing a piece with a pro hockey player."

"Doesn't that make it all the better?" he says, and I picture Cade waggling his eyebrows.

I don't hate the idea of Dwayne seeing his daughter playing piano with Cade. It would make him wonder who Cade is to me. Not that it will make him jealous, of course. He moved on from me a long time ago.

Wait. This is not a smart idea. It would be totally unprofessional of me to say yes for the exact same reason why it would feel good for Dwayne to witness.

"I really appreciate you making the offer, Cade, but I'm sorry, it can't happen."

"Why not? I told you it's not against the rules."

"It's so sweet of you to offer, let alone check the rules on this competition, but—"

"But nothing."

"This is a small town, Cade. People talk. Dwayne will assume you and I are..." I trail off, hoping he'll catch my drift and not make me say it outright.

"He'll assume what, Triple?"

It would seem he *is* going to make me say it outright.

"Involved."

"Involved? How would that look exactly?" His teasing tone sends a tingle down my spine.

"You know exactly how that would look and it's not appropriate. We work together."

"That's it. I'll quit."

A laugh bursts out of me. "You'll quit?"

"Why not? Sure, I'm the best right winger the team's got and I'm a massive playmaker, racking those points up on the scoreboard for my team every week with goals and assists. But they'll survive without me. Eventually."

"You're impossible, did you know that?"

"Impossible or irresistible?"

I shake my head, laughing once more. "I think you're so sweet to want to do this for Hannah, but I think I'm going to have to say no."

"Come on. It'll be great for her. You know it will."

I twist my mouth. He has a point. Hannah is determined to perform in this talent show, but she's also inexperienced in piano and is already super nervous about it, and it's not even until the week before Thanksgiving. What's more, the chemistry she had with Cade when they were playing "Chopsticks" together was undeniable, and it was wonderful to see her playing and smiling, enjoying herself.

After what happened with her skating recital, I know being up on the stage with someone she likes and trusts could really help her overcome this newfound stage fright, and Lord knows I couldn't fulfill that role for her, what with being a musical talent wasteland.

"Let me think about it," I concede.

"I'll give you five seconds from now. Five, four, three—"

"Were you an overindulged child?"

"Two, one. What's your decision?"

"Cade," I warn.

"Okay. I'll back off. But will you at least think about it?"

"I'll think about it."

"Good."

There's a silence between us, and I find I don't want to hang up on this man.

"Cade?"

"What is it, Triple?"

"You're a good guy."

"Don't go telling anyone that. I've got a reputation to uphold. Or to smash. One or the other. See you at the arena Monday?"

"Monday?"

"You know, the Ice Breakers? It's this new NHL team we both work for? They push a small black object around a rink, trying to slot it into a net?"

I chortle. "Yeah. I remember."

"You're filming after practice, right? That's what Coach Hauser told us at practice today."

He's right. I've got a few guys lined up to do some trick shots at the end of practice tomorrow morning, which I'm filming for a new campaign. With the success of the TikTok involving Cade, Asher, and Weston which I posted after the livestream, Veronica has requested more dancing, too, so I'll be looking for more volunteers. Asher told me that he's a shoo-in.

Plus, there's the fact Veronica wants videos of just Cade and me, which frankly, I've been putting off filming. Being around Cade is challenging enough without it all being caught on camera.

But I do need to capture the content, so I reply, "Let's film the first Hockey 101 video tomorrow after the trick shots."

"You got it, Triple," he replies, and I can hear the delight in his voice.

"Good night, Cade."

"Night, Triple. Sweet dreams."

The call ends and it's obvious to me he wants my sweet dreams to be about him.

Little does he know they may well be.

CHAPTER 11
CADE

THE ICE of the arena is gleaming under the stark lights, my breath visible as I expel air from my lungs. Coach has already run us through a bunch of conditioning drills over the last hour or more, and my hair's dripping with sweat, plastered to my forehead under my helmet.

This morning's training has been tough, even tougher than I'm used to. But then everyone on this team has got something to prove, Coach Hauser included, and I'm here for it, every last drill. I want this team to be a success just as much as anyone, and I'm not afraid to put in the work to achieve that goal.

"I want everyone off the ice except Hayes, Simpson, and Crane in offense, and Lowe and Smith on defense!" Coach yells in his raspy voice, and I heave a sigh of relief, knowing I'll be getting at least a couple minutes respite from today's grueling training.

Always ready to lead, Jamie begins to demonstrate the three on two drill with Nate and Carson, up against the defensive pairing of Lucian and Weston. Coach yells out instructions, and we watch from the bench, analyzing the defenders' positioning.

"That guy. He needs to improve his defensive stance," Clément says in his French accent, catching his breath along with the rest of us.

"Who?" I ask.

"Lucian Lowe. Look."

I watch Lucian as he rushes the offense, looking strong and quick out there on the ice as far as I can see.

I'm about to ask him what he means when Coach yells, "Next line! Lennox, Tremblay, go join Hayes. Simpson and Crane, you're off. You're up against Lowe and Smith. Get out there and show me something creative. Lennox, you're leading the rush."

"You got it, Coach!" I yell and spring into action despite my tiredness.

Man, I love it when I get to lead.

Quickly, we get ourselves into formation at center ice. We form a quick huddle to strategize the play.

"I've got an idea. Let's run that cross-and-drop we've been working on," I say, and my new buddy Asher nods enthusiastically.

"I'll take the high slot if you draw Lowe wide," he says.

Asher spins his stick. "And I'll be waiting at the backdoor, like a thief in the night."

"Just be ready for the pass," Jamie says.

Coach blows the whistle, and I glide back to the blue line, ready to rush as I notice Lucian and Weston pulling apart from their defensive play discussion.

I was brought into this team for my solid offensive skills, and I need to keep proving that I'm worth every cent.

Lucian is watching me with the intensity of a leopard watching its prey, and Weston taps his stick on the ice.

It's *on*.

I burst into action, transitioning the puck from forehand to backhand as I build speed through the neutral zone. I'm flanked by Asher as Jamie creates some space on my other side as the defensive pair backs away, ready.

I pass to Asher who ploughs ahead toward the goal, receiving the puck cleanly before he returns it to me in the blink of an eye.

"Keep it tight!" Coach shouts.

Accelerating forward, I'm now in space with Lucian, with Asher positioned at the back, his stick ready if I can thread the needle. It's a classic textbook setup, the kind of offensive play that made me a star on the Blades.

Time seems to slow as I look for the perfect moment to shoot. I raise my stick just as the heavy doors to the players' entrance swing open, and I spot a splash of red against the monotone of the arena.

It's Clara, looking particularly hot in a red fitted blazer and skirt, her blonde hair in a bun catching the light.

And that's all it takes, one moment of distraction and the puck is stolen from me by Lucian with impeccable timing. He delivers a perfect hip check that catches me out and my body becomes momentarily airborne before I come crashing down to the ice, my stick sliding away from me.

Coach blows his whistle and yells, "Stop!"

"What the heck, Lennox?" Jamie says as he comes to a stop at my side, ice chips flying.

"You okay, man?" Asher asks, offering me his hand, pulling me back up to my feet.

"Yeah," I reply, more humiliated that I allowed my concentration to slip than anything else.

From the boards, Clément calls out, "*Oh la la*! This man was annihilated!"

Helpful, Frenchie.

I push into a skate, trying to outrun my humiliation before the three of us huddle once more.

"What the heck happened?" Jamie asks.

"He decided to take a little nap mid-rush. Right, Lennox?" Asher says with a slap to my back.

"Something like that," I mutter under my breath as I brush ice from my chest, sliding my eyes to Clara. She's watching me with concern written across her face, and a fresh wave of humiliation rolls over me.

Jamie looks between Clara and me, his expression telling me he's worked out this particular equation. "Save it for after practice, Romeo. 'Kay?"

"Got it, Captain," I murmur.

Asher pats me on the butt as he skates back into position, and I throw him an embarrassed smile.

Clément skates past us, heading to the net. "Love makes fools of all of us, *mon ami*."

Both Jamie and Asher bark out a laugh, Asher turning to smile at Clara.

Great. Now everyone on the team knows I've got a fat crush on the social media manager.

I steal one final glance at Clara. She's now setting up her camera, and all I can do is hope she's blissfully unaware that she's the reason I just performed an unintentional aerial routine.

A few moves—and thankfully a goal on my behalf—later and Coach has us lined up dishing out individual feedback.

"Lennox, you need to be locked in every second you're on the ice," he says, and there's a rumble of laughter from the team.

"Won't happen again, Coach," I say, *not* looking in Clara's direction. Which is hard because she looks so dang good, this time her skirt hitting just above her knees, and man, her legs are long and slim and perfect.

But I can't lose focus just because the girl I've got feelings for has walked in. That's *never* happened to me before. Not even once. And I've had plenty of women I've been involved with watching my games.

But then I guess I've never felt this way about someone before, and I've got no clue how to deal with it.

The old me would have seduced Clara by now. Gotten her out of my system. But the thing is, I don't want Clara out of my system.

And the thought makes something move in my chest.

"Clara here wants to film some trick shots for social media," he says, gesturing at her. "Clara? What did you have in mind?"

"Thanks, Coach Hauser, and it's great to see you all again," she begins, a spot of feminine beauty amongst all the sweat and testosterone.

"Some of us are falling over, we're so happy to see you. Isn't that right, Lennox?" Weston says, winning laughs from the team —and a glare from me.

So *not* funny.

Clara's eyes dart between me and Weston, but to her credit, she doesn't bite. Hope springs that she doesn't know I took a fall because of her.

"I'm here to film some trick shots, as you know, but first I want to take the opportunity to talk about the Drench for Defense coming up at the farmers' market this weekend. Thank you to Weston, Carson, Asher, and Cade for volunteering for it so far. If anyone else wants to join, please let me know today. The more the merrier when it comes to this kind of event, and the more money we can raise to save the town, the better."

"I guess I should do it as team captain," Jamie says.

"Thank you, Jamie! Having the captain will be an amazing addition," Clara replies. "Now, you'll be glad to know I don't plan on taking too much of your time today, but I do have a full team trick shot series I've got in mind. It's called a domino derby."

"I know those. You start with one guy who does a trick shot and then passes to the next who does another until we've done the whole team across," Lucian says.

"You got it," Clara replies. "Sound okay to you guys?"

Some of the guys shrug, some grunt, and a couple reply with "sure."

"Loving that enthusiasm," she says with a dollop of sarcasm.

"Ms. Johnson isn't doing this for fun, men. This will help get new fans, and a new team in the League needs new fans. Isn't that correct?" Coach says.

"Coach Hauser is absolutely right, and trick shots are trending right now on social media, so I'd love all your help," she says.

"You got it," I say, knowing I'll get endless ribbing in the locker room after. "Right, guys?"

My team murmurs their agreement, and Clara throws me a grateful smile.

Worth it.

"All right. Let's go ahead with the full team, and then if there's anyone who would like to stick around to do some individual trick shots, that would be awesome."

"I know one person who'll wanna stick around," Weston says, and several of the team snort with laughter.

"*Ah, l'amour,*" Clément adds, his hand on his heart, and I shove his shoulder.

To her credit, Clara glosses over it, acting totally professional as she organizes us into a line across the ice. For someone so small, she's surprisingly skilled at bossing us big guys around.

We pass the puck between us, and she takes us through a practice run of her domino derby before she begins to film.

I start by shooting the puck to ricochet off Lucian's stick, who redirects it to Carson, who banks it off the boards, coming within inches of Weston's helmet, sending it careening toward Clément, who adds a dramatic flourish before Jamie catches it mid-air and flips it into the up before passing it to Asher. The tricks continue until all the guys on the team have added their particular flair, and the mood shifts from post-practice exhaustion to an atmosphere of fun.

"That's so great, guys!" Clara exclaims as she watches us. "I've got what I need with this one. Do I have any volunteers for some small group or singular trick shots?"

Several of the guys volunteer, excited to show off their skills, including Asher and Clément. I put my hand up, too, receiving knowing smirks from the team.

"Shocker," Weston says under his breath, and Lucian snorts.

But I don't care. So what if the guys know I've got a thing for Clara. That's our business, no one else's. And it's not like anything has happened between us.

Even though I want it to, more and more each day.

Most of the team hits the showers, leaving me, Asher, and Clément with Clara.

"I have the most amazing trick for you, *mademoiselle*. I call it the French Kiss," Clément says before he skates toward one of the nets.

Of course he does. That guy is as French as they get. I half expect to hear accordion music playing whenever he's around, the scent of croissants in the air.

Clara lifts her phone, ready to capture his trick. Clément flips the puck in a perfect arc before it drops onto the crossbar, bouncing off of it, at which point he slaps it into the net.

"Where's the french kiss in that?" Asher calls out, and Clément skates back to us.

"The puck delicately kissed the bar before hitting its target, like a man in love kissing his woman," Clément explains in his typically French, poetic way.

"I guess that one takes some imagination. Am I right?" Asher says, and he fist bumps me.

"I thought it was awesome, Clément," Clara says, shooting us her mom look, like we're a couple of naughty kids.

Is it terrible that I find that super hot?

Probably.

"Whose turn is it next?" she asks.

"Mine," I say as I slide the puck from Clément and position it near the boards, lining up my shot. I'm ready to do a trick I've been performing since high school, one that has never failed to impress.

I can only hope Clara notices.

And yes, I know how tragic that sounds to use an old high school hockey trick to try to win her over. But impressing Clara has quickly risen to the top of my list of goals in this new town.

As my stick makes contact with the puck, I send it ricocheting toward the goal, where I chase it and slot it into the target. Then, I flick the puck up in the air and balance it on my blade while skating backwards, flicking it over my shoulder into the net once more, only this time without even looking.

Satisfied with not one but two tricks, I skate back to Clara.

"Double the genius," Asher exclaims appreciatively. "Respect, man."

"It's no french kiss, but it was skillful," Clément concedes.

"Impressive," Clara says, and her beautiful smile makes heat spread through my chest.

What can I say? The trick works. Every. Single. Time.

It's Asher's turn next and he grabs three pucks and a helmet before he skates to center ice.

"Dude! What do you need three pucks for?" I call out.

"Watch and learn, my friend. Watch and learn," he replies with a smug smile.

I lean back, confident he can't top my double trick. But in a matter of seconds, he's done just that, flipping pucks off his stick, catching them mid-air like they're pancakes and sending them flying into the helmet positioned on the ice, which spins each time a puck lands inside it.

As he returns to the boards, I give him a slow clap like he's in a 90s movie, and he takes a theatrical bow that's more Clément's style than his.

"The deepest respect," Clément says, bowing back.

"Yeah, man. That was awesome," I tell him and give him a fist bump.

"Better than yours?" Asher asks, and I give a begrudging nod.

"Yeah, better than mine."

"You guys were all amazing. Thank you so much for this," Clara says, tapping her phone.

"Will you tag us individually when you share them?" Asher asks.

"Of course. Our followers are going to love these." Clara clicks her phone off. "Cade, we need to do another video, if you have the time?"

"Sure thing," I reply.

Clément smirks. "You are enthusiastic when it comes to social media, *non*?"

"Yeah, Lennox. Why *is* that?" Asher asks and wins the side eye from me.

He knows exactly why.

"My boss thinks Cade and I work well together on camera," Clara explains, and I raise my brows at the guys as if to say *See? Totally legit.*

"We're doing the Hockey 101 video, right?" I ask Clara.

"That's right. Kind of like hockey for dummies," she explains.

"Oh, Cade's your man, for sure. He practically defines the word 'dummy,'" Asher teases.

"Whatever," I say with a good-humored shake of my head.

"I'm looking forward to seeing you at Drench for Defense this Saturday, Asher. Are you sure I can't persuade you to join us, Clément?" Clara asks.

"I don't like to have water thrown at me," he sniffs.

"Dude, it's not like *we* like it," I say, but all he does is say *au revoir* and head toward the locker room.

"Thanks again for volunteering, you two. The forecast looks mild enough and sunny, you'll be glad to know."

"We're hockey players. We're used to the cold," I assure her.

"Yeah, but we don't usually have buckets of water thrown at us," Asher replies. "We wear our game day gear for the event, right?"

"That's right, plus a change of clothes. We'll supply towels and hot chocolate afterwards to warm you back up in the tent," she says.

"You got it, Clara. Enjoy your *video*," Asher says, emphasizing the word before he throws me a look and leaves.

I pull the door open and step off the ice. Towering over Clara due to the fact I'm almost a foot taller than her plus my skates, I sit, and she does the same.

"You're looking especially good today, Triple. Red's your color."

"That's nice of you to say," she replies.

I shrug. "I just say it like it is."

"Look, I want to say something that's been playing on my mind."

"You feel this thing too?" I reply, only half joking, because it's obvious she does, even if she insists on fighting it.

"I'm being serious here. I wanted to offer once again to pay you for the toy you gave Benny. It's only right."

I hold my hands in the air. "I already said it's a gift, and it's not a toy. It's a collectible."

"But—" she protests.

"Seriously. It's a gift. End of story."

She lets out a defeated breath. "It's so generous of you. You're very kind to give it to him."

"Yeah, I am," I say with a grin, and she lets out a laugh.

"And modest. Did I mention that?"

"Just another dip layer, Triple. Is Hannah coming over for piano practice tomorrow?"

She scrunches her nose. "I don't know it's a good idea, you know, with her dad coming to Show Quest."

"Why would that be a problem?"

"I'm pretty sure he wouldn't like another man performing with his daughter."

I'm itching to say that I'm sure *she* didn't like it when her ex ran off with her best friend, but that didn't stop the guy.

Instead, I concede, "That's fine. I get it. I don't want to rock the boat."

"Thank you," she replies, her features relaxing.

"I'm still happy to help her get ready for the competition, though."

"You are? You're so—"

"Amazing? Incredible? *Hot*?" I suggest with my cheesiest of grins, which makes her smile.

"Kind. That's the word I was going for."

"I'll take it. We can work on the others later." I throw her a wink, and she barks out another laugh, this time shaking her head.

"You never quit, do you?"

"Not when it comes to you, Triple. Take me or leave me." I lean closer to her, catching her scent, and say in an intimate tone, "Only I suggest you take me."

I waggle my brows at her, and she laughs once more, and I decide there and then that hearing Clara Johnson laugh is the most wonderful sound in the world.

CHAPTER 12
CLARA

VERONICA'S DIRECTIVE WAS CLEAR. Create content featuring me interacting with Cade on camera, oozing the "chemistry" she insists she sees between us.

Well, her and half the social media commenting population, that is.

I admit, it's hard not to agree with her when I look at the accidental livestream that started this whole thing. There's a certain tension between us when we look into one another's eyes. It's intense, the moment stretching for a beat too long as he holds me close to him, my limbs melting like honey against his firm frame.

If only I hadn't agreed to the dance in the first place. If only Joel hadn't mistakenly thought I'd told him to livestream it.

But these things happened, and I need to step up and do what my boss has told me to do—even if it feels a lot like walking right into the lion's den—and the lion is most definitely Cade Lennox and that flirty grin that zips straight through me like a live wire.

Just to confuse things more, there's Veronica's second directive ringing in my ears. Watch out for Cade Lennox with his heartbreaker rep.

I blow out a breath. This is like walking a tightrope. One wrong step and I'm done, either losing my job or losing my head with Cade.

Neither of the things are on my To Do list right now.

"So, Hockey 101. What do you want to know?" he asks.

"Well," I manage, trying to sound like a serious content creator rather than someone whose professional objectivity always seems to melt around this guy. "How about we start with something basic? Like the rules of the game, but not in a dry way."

"Triple, there's nothing dry about me."

I swallow, the way his eyes bore into mine raising my temperature. "Good to know. Let's start with what a faceoff is and then move onto other terms."

"Happy to."

I set up the tripod, my fingers fumbling with the equipment, intensely aware of his eyes tracking my every move. "Why don't you grab your stick and a puck and skate out onto the ice a little and I'll get you in frame?"

"Sure thing," he replies as he rises to his impossible height, stepping through the door, and gliding across the ice. He turns to look at me. "Is here good, Triple?"

"A little closer. And don't call me Triple on camera, okay?"

"Sure thing, *Clara.*"

He shifts closer to the camera, and I call out, "Stop! Perfect.

Let me get my skates on, and I'll join you in a sec. Don't move. Got it?"

He salutes me, his grin wide. "Yes, ma'am!"

I tilt my head to the side and throw him a look.

"Too soon?" he asks with a shrug, his boyish charm oozing right out of him.

"Too soon," I reply as I sit down and concentrate on lacing up my skates.

A moment later, I press record, step onto the ice, and cover the short distance to him.

"Hey, you're good at this," he says.

"Not my first rodeo. I grew up around this arena. I spent many hours here skating around to music with my friends."

"Tell me it was in a little figure skating costume with one of those tiny skirts at your hips."

I roll my eyes at him. "Seriously, Cade?"

He holds his hands up. "What can I say? Flirting with you is too fun to resist."

"Try harder."

"I make no promises."

I turn to the camera and begin. "I'm here with Cade Lennox, star winger of the newest team in the League, the Ice Breakers, and a player I know you all love. Cade's going to take us through some hockey basics in this, our first Hockey 101 video." I turn to him. "Cade, tell us about the tools you use as a hockey player."

"This," he says, brandishing his stick at the camera. "This is a hockey stick. It's what we players use to push a little black disc around the ice." He holds up the puck. "And this is that little black disc, aka the puck or the biscuit, as we players tend to call it."

His personality shines through and I know we're off to a good start.

"So you push a puck around the ice, trying to get it into your opposition's net to score points. Correct?"

"There's a little bit more to it than that, Clara," he says with a laugh.

"Nice segue to some of the questions I've got from the public." I pull a folded piece of paper from my jacket pocket and read the first line. "Selena from Seattle says she knows nothing about hockey and only watches it for the hot guys." Cade laughs. "She wants you to explain the positions on the team."

"Happy to, Selena. There are three forwards, two defensemen, and one goalie on a team. Forwards are centers and wingers, like me, and we make things happen on the ice."

"So you're saying you're a troublemaker?" I ask.

"Me?" he asks innocently. "Centers are like the quarterbacks of hockey. They take the faceoffs and distribute the puck. Wingers like me support the center and try to create scoring opportunities. So yeah, it's kinda our job to create trouble for the opposition as we try to get the points on the board."

"What about the defense?" I ask, happy with the direction the interview is going so far.

"The defense is like the responsible older siblings. They keep us from getting into too much trouble. Like you and me." He waggles his brows at me, and I can't help but smile.

"Moving onto the next question. Lauren from Tacoma wants to know what a faceoff is, and why it's got that name."

"A faceoff is where two players line up, face to face, sticks on the ice." He positions his stick between us. "The ref drops the puck right between the two players like this." He drops the puck onto the ice, the dense rubber landing with a sharp *click*. He lifts his head, his eyes locked on mine with an intensity that seems to have absolutely nothing to do with the rules of hockey. "And then it's all about who wants it more. Who can read the other person's intentions and react faster. It's about knowing exactly when to make your move."

I press my lips together, his low voice rumbling over me. Why does this feel like it's about more than just hockey?

"Because if you hesitate, if you second-guess yourself for even one second, someone else wins control."

I clear my throat, like that'll help me pretend his words didn't just knock my equilibrium sideways. "And what happens when someone wins that control?" I ask.

"You get to decide what happens next. You get to make all the plays. Of course, sometimes the real strategy is letting the other person think they're winning, right up until you make your move."

His words drip in innuendo, and I'm beginning to wonder why I ever agreed to doing this with him.

"So, Lauren," I say, facing the camera, which feels way safer than looking into Cade's eyes as his words roll over me. "It turns out faceoffs are super strategic."

"Everything in hockey is strategic. You need to read the other players, know when to be patient, and when to be aggressive." He pauses for a beat. "When to go for what you really want."

Oh, this is definitely not just about hockey anymore.

I should have known he'd be like this, all suggestive and... *Cade*. But I've got to give the people what they want, and they want to see that chemistry between us once more. So, I steel myself to ask my next question from the list.

"Deanna from Spokane wants to know what a slapshot is," I ask, noticing that all my questions seem to be from women.

"That's easy. A slapshot is when a player winds up and whacks the puck with major force instead of just nudging it around the ice. It's a definitive move and can change the play in a second."

That's better. A straight answer. No innuendo, no flirtation.

We are back on track.

"And of course a slapshot could create a scoring opportunity," he adds.

A*aaaa*nd we're back to flirty again.

"Creating scoring opportunities are all about patience and positioning," Cade continues, this time looking at the camera.

"You can't force it, even if you want to. You have to wait for the perfect setup."

"How do you know when the moment's right?"

He nudges the puck with his stick skillfully on the ice as he speaks. "You learn to read the signs, you know? The defense might shift, and maybe an opening appears at the perfect time. Sometimes you get just one shot, and other times you get a bunch in a row. It's unpredictable like that."

"And when you finally get that perfect opportunity?" I ask, quite possibly against my better judgment.

"You put everything you've got behind it." His gaze is positively smoldering now as it lands on mine. "Because missing a perfect scoring opportunity is something you regret for a long, long time."

Lord, have mercy.

I'm going to have to edit this video to within an inch of its life.

That's it. I've reached my limit with this flirty talk that's sending tingles through me and making me think of things other than hockey. "Cade, can you be serious for even one minute?"

"You know me. I'm always serious, Triple," he says with a grin that says the exact opposite.

"You're being all flirty and suggestive. Let's just concentrate on hockey, okay?"

He opens his mouth to speak, and I hold my finger up. "And don't tell me you were concentrating solely on hockey, because we both know you weren't."

He nudges me with his elbow. "Come on. Even you can admit this is fun."

I twist my mouth. With his easygoing and playful nature, Cade can make me feel like I'm seriously uptight, too strait-laced to have fun. Which isn't true. I can have fun along with the best of them. The problem is, letting go of this tight control I have on myself around him could lead to places I don't want to go.

Places I *can't* go, not if I want to honor the non-fraternization clause in my contract and keep my sanity.

Because I know I could so easily give in to this man with his sexy grin and smoldering eyes. Because Cade is so much more than that. He's got substance. Depth. He's kind and patient and cares deeply for those people lucky enough to be in his life.

I could fall for a man like Cade Lennox, and I can't let that happen, even if the terrible truth is, I think I already am falling for him.

The plan was simple: do my job, create engaging content, prove I belong in this professional world I've worked so hard to be a part of. It didn't include developing feelings for a player whose reputation precedes him like a warning siren.

Except I know that's only part of who he is, and getting to know the real Cade, the man behind the carefree, flirty façade? Well, that might just be my undoing.

Even if the way he's looking at me right now suggests he's worth the risk.

CHAPTER 13
CLARA

I'M PREPARING to knock on Cade's polished wooden door when it swings open, revealing Cade in all his Cade-ness. Which is to say he's wearing casual clothes that show off his wide shoulders and long legs, and his characteristically broad smile.

I'm hit with a sudden, unhelpful flutter at the sight of him, and I count my blessings he's got a top on, covering his muscular frame.

"Hey, it's my favorite little Maple Leafers," he exclaims as he grins at my kids.

Benny giggles.

"We're not maple leaves. We're people," Hannah insists.

He narrows his eyes as though to assess them both. "You are too. My bad. She's a smart one," he says to me.

"Oh, yes," I reply.

"Come on in." He stands back for the three of us to enter.

We hang our jackets on the hooks by the door, and make our way into the living room, Benny chatting incessantly about *The Timekeeper Chronicles*.

"Owen said it's so cool! Max helps a Forgotten Girl do her dragon book report and he fixes time," Benny says.

"And that's in the new comic book you say?" Cade asks as we reach his open plan living-slash-kitchen. There's a delicious aroma in the air, like we've walked into an Italian restaurant.

"Sure is. Mommy, can we go get it from Aunt Emmy's store tomorrow? Please?" Benny pleads.

"I've got the Drench for Defense at the farmers' market tomorrow, buddy. We can go one day after school next week," I reply.

He tries again. "Please?"

"Next week, sweetheart. I promise," I say.

Benny lowers his head and kicks the ground. "Okay."

"How about I save you the trip?" Cade asks, and Benny's head suddenly pings up as Cade pulls a comic book from behind his back.

Benny grabs for it, his eyes wide. "This is the latest comic book! Mommy, did you see this?"

"I see it, Benny, and it's so nice of Cade to let you read his," I reply.

"This one's for him. I'll get another copy from Falling for Books tomorrow after the Drench for Defense," he replies.

"Oh, no," I say in protest. "Benny can just read it here. At the table, Benny, and be super careful with it. Okay?"

"Okay, Mommy," he says absentmindedly, his nose already deep in the comic book pages as he slips onto one of Cade's dining room chairs.

"Benny's so lucky," Hannah says with a sigh. She's clearly

fishing, and I'm about to tell her off for doing so when Cade cuts in.

"Don't worry, Hannah. I got something for everyone, plus I've got a lasagna in the oven for after."

"Cade," I warn, but it's too late as he produces a sparkly blue figure skating dress for Hannah, whose eyes bulge at the sight of it.

"For me?" she asks eagerly.

"Well, I originally got it for me, but it was a size too small," Cade says with a grin, and I can't help but laugh, despite the fact he's continuing to spoil my kids.

"Thank you! Can I go try it on, Mommy? Please?" she asks, tilting her excited little face my way.

"Of course you can," I reply, but she's already taking off through the living room.

"The bathroom is the second door on your right," Cade calls after her, and next thing we hear is the *thunk* of a door closing.

"Cade, you shouldn't have," I say, but all he does is shrug.

"I wanted to. I got something for you, too."

"Cade—"

"Let me do this, Triple, okay? Gift giving is my love language."

Love language? At the mention of the "L" word, I clamp my mouth shut, my heart doing weird things in my chest.

Of course I don't love Cade. I've only known him for a matter of weeks, and besides, he and I are so very different. He's all flirty and charming and carefree, a guy at the top of his chosen career. Life might not be perfect for him, but he's living it to its fullest, and making it look easy.

Me? I'm a single mom doing my best to raise two kids with only sporadic help from their father. I'm working hard to establish myself in a new job while navigating the complexity of an online relationship with someone I'm no longer sure I have feelings for. At the same time, I'm developing some serious feelings for someone much closer to home—the man whose kitchen I'm standing in right now.

I know I'm falling for him, but I also know he has the power to break my heart in two.

Then there's the fact that he doesn't have a non-fraternization clause in his contract, and if he did, he's probably not the kind of guy to give it a second thought. But I do, and that clause is enough reason for me to at least *try* keep this thing between us platonic, even if he's worming his way into my affections more and more every day.

Before I got to see the real Cade, it was so much easier than this. Before, all I had to contend with was my physical attraction for the guy, which I could put down to the fact that he's classically handsome and has this boyish charm and confident swagger that's really quite disarming. That's just surface level, aspects of a person that might attract you at the start but mean so much less as you get to know the real person. Who they are and what makes them tick. Their values. Their priorities. Their soul.

Now? Way harder. He's still got all the good looks and boyish charm, but he's so much more than just that. He's got heart. Depth.

And he's made his intentions toward me crystal clear.

"Here." He pushes a pale pink box twice the size of a shoebox toward me.

I glance at him as I pull at the ribbon, my heart going all kinds of crazy. As I lift the lid, I see a pair of thick, cozy socks, a tube of expensive organic hand cream, a packet of organic chamomile tea, some lip balm, and a bottle of lavender oil.

"It's a care package because you mentioned that sometimes you find it hard to unwind after your busy days, and I know how important it is for people with chronic conditions to look after themselves, as Dr. Bernice reminded us all at this week's support group."

If I thought my heart was going all kinds of crazy before,

that's nothing compared with what it's doing now. Handsome, athletic, charming, and capable of giving thoughtful gifts?

You are not playing fair, Universe.

And this isn't just some generic bunch of flowers like Dwayne used to give me in the early days of our relationship. This is thoughtful, a gift he put time into. One that means so much to me.

"Cade, I...I don't know what to say."

"Reserve your judgment until you look at what's underneath," he instructs, and I do as he says, lifting the items to reveal a soft, folded blanket in a pretty lemon color.

I run my hand over it, feeling its plushness, Cade's thoughtfulness hitting me hard in the solar plexus.

"It's a weighted blanket. I got one for my mom a while back, and she said it really helps her feel calm and secure at night, which means she sleeps better. I thought you might like one."

Sudden warmth spreads through my chest like sunlight breaking through clouds, and to my mortification, my eyes pool with tears, and I can barely catch my breath.

"Hey. What's wrong?" Cade asks softly, stepping closer to me and placing his hand over mine.

I try to swallow the lump in my throat, sniffing back the unexpected—and definitely uninvited—tears. "It's...it's just—" I begin, the rawness in my voice catching me unaware. "You're so thoughtful." I look up into his eyes and see compassion and understanding.

"Sometimes we all need to be looked after, Triple."

"I have people who look after me. Keira and Dan are amazing, and they help me with the kids and everything, and the Chronic Warriors? They give me so much support and practical help. So, I'm lucky. I'm really, really lucky. I don't know why I'm feeling so emotional right now." I'm babbling as I wipe away an errant tear that has slid down my cheek.

Cade places his big hands on either side of my arms, now so close to me I can breathe in his masculine scent. "You're an amazing mom, you're holding down a new full-time job that you're killing at, and you've got to work with arrogant jocks like me."

"You're not an arrogant jock," I reply, my voice only just above a whisper.

"You thought I was when we first met. No, wait. You thought I was a pedophile."

I snort laugh and quickly cover my mouth with my hand.

"You're doing great. Let somebody take care of you." He lifts his lips in a small smile that makes his eyes twinkle. "And by 'somebody' you know I mean me, right?"

I let out a watery laugh, moving my hand to my chest where my heart is beating fast. "I figured." I suck in a ragged breath. "You're so not who I thought you were, Cade Lennox."

He smiles down, and I feel every one of the extra inches he has on me. "I think you've already told me that."

"You keep showing me, and I'm so grateful. Thank you for this. It means a lot."

"Look, Clara, I—" he begins, only for Hannah to choose that very moment to come dancing into the room in her new sparkly dress, looking every inch the figure skating princess.

"Mommy! Mommy! Look at me!" she calls as she twirls and pirouettes across the living room floor.

"Very pretty, sweetheart," I say, pulling back from Cade and clasping my hands together as I watch her.

I blink back my tears, but something has shifted inside me. Those tears were real, honest, brought on by Cade's genuine thoughtfulness. This moment between us feels like something I'll carry with me, something I'll turn over in my mind again and again.

I watch him grin at Hannah as she prances around the room, and the truth hits me like a physical blow. This isn't just about the gifts—though seeing him choose something perfect for both of my kids and for me does something dangerous to my heart. It's watching him see us in a way Dwayne never bothered to.

There's the non-fraternization policy, sure. But that's not what has begun to terrify me. What terrifies me is remembering how Dwayne loved me and then walked away without a backward glance, leaving not just me but Hannah and Benny, too.

How he made both me and our kids feel disposable.

I can't do that to them again. I can't let them get attached to someone who might leave. And a rich, successful hockey player, a man adored by fans across the country, a man who has his pick of women, could so easily change his mind about us. Anyone with half a brain could tell me that.

But then I watch Cade crouch down to Hannah's level, asking her to show him her best spin, and something inside me cracks open.

I'd convinced myself I was falling for Warrior, safe and distant, a man who could never really hurt us because he'd never really be here.

Only I was lying to myself.

Because standing here, watching Cade with my kids, feeling the echo of his hand on mine, I can't deny it anymore. The warmth spreading through my chest, the way my breath catches when he looks at me, the way everything in me reaches toward him despite every rational thought screaming at me to stop?

I'm falling for Cade Lennox, and I think I'm ready to stop fighting it.

CHAPTER 14
CADE

WHAT COULD BE MORE small-town quaint than a farmers' market on a Saturday morning, brimming with locals and delicious smells wafting in the air, the leaves of the surrounding trees lit up in red, gold, and orange? I wander past the stands selling everything from fresh produce to cured meats to waffles with maple syrup and cream. And yes, I'm sorely tempted to get one of those delicious smelling waffles, but Coach has the team on a strict diet, and last time I checked, waffles with maple syrup and cream weren't on the list.

I do take a mental note to come back here once the season is done and buy the whole stand's worth. Man, it smells good.

The barista at the coffee cart calls my name and I thank her as I collect the coffees I got for me and Clara before I head across the grass to the Drench for Defense tent.

"Well, hello, Cade Lennox," says a petite woman over sixty, with short-cropped gray hair, and glasses.

"Nice to meet you, ma'am," I reply with a respectful nod of my head.

"Oh, forget calling me ma'am," she says with a wave of her hand. "Mary-Ellen McCluskey. I'm Mabel's mom and I live on the same street as you, right across from Clara and Ashlyn." She puts her hand on my forearm. "Oh, my, what fine arms you have, Mr. Lennox."

"Thank you, Mrs. McCluskey," I reply because what else can I say?

"Are you doing the Soaked for Safety thing today? Or is it Buckets Against Bulldozers? Whatever it's called, everyone's talking about it, and I know quite a few of us locals who are excited to participate."

"That's great to hear." I point at the banner across the grass that proclaims the event's name. "It's Drench for Defense. You see, it's got a double meaning: defense in hockey and defending the town against the developers."

"Oh, isn't that clever? Who came up with that?"

I can't stop my smile from forming. "I think it was Clara Johnson."

"Clara? Oh, isn't she a sweetheart? And we're all so proud of her getting that new job of hers after everything she's been through."

"Yeah," I agree, my chest tightening as I think of Clara last night. The way her eyes shimmered with tears over a simple gift. How badly I wanted to cup her face and kiss those tears away, telling her everything I've been holding back. That somewhere between her eye rolls at my terrible jokes and watching her fierce protectiveness with her kids, I'm falling for her.

Last night, I'd planned to say it all. Had the words lined up like a perfect play call on the ice.

Then Hannah pirouetted into the room in her full sparkly glory, and the moment morphed into lasagna and piano practice and Clara herding her kids out the door.

And here's the thing about kids—they commandeer every moment, turning what might have been intimate confessions into family sitcoms without missing a beat.

Most guys would find that inconvenient, but for me, it's exactly why I'm falling so hard for all three of them.

Mary-Ellen McCluskey leans closer to me, giving my arm a squeeze. "Did you know Clara Johnson's got the GPS?"

I shoot her a confused look. "The GPS?"

She pulls her brows together. "Or is it the CBS? Yes, that's it. She's got the CBS."

I bite back a smile. Clara isn't a TV station or global positioning software. "Chronic fatigue. CFS. Yeah, I know."

"I blame that ex-husband of hers. Dwayne Campbell. Horrible man. You know she changed her name back to her maiden name after he did what he did? I do not blame her one little bit. He ran off with her dear friend, Izzy, you know, *and* he's from Oregon." She throws me a knowing look, and it's not clear which is the worse crime in her book: running off with Clara's friend or being from out of state.

"Well, it's been nice to see you, Mrs. McCluskey. I need to get ready for my drenching now. Be sure to stop by and bid on one of the guys. Who knows, you might win the chance to throw a bucket of water over one of us."

Her eyes are shining. "I'm volunteering for the event, so I'll see you there." She gives my arm a final squeeze before she lets go of me and I make my way toward the tent.

"Lennox! Over here!" a voice calls and I spot Asher grinning under the overhead banner that announces "Drench for

Defense" in bold blue lettering, under which is the subheading that claims, "Drench Your Favorite Ice Breaker to Save Maple Falls."

No one ever tells you when you make it onto the League that hockey can lead to a bunch of weird stuff.

But you know what? I believe in this town I now call home, and if getting a bucket of water thrown over me by the paying public is me playing my small part, then I say bring it on. This town has a life to it, a vibe I connect with, a slower pace of life that feels right to me at the grand old age of thirty-three. Even though the entire town could fit inside a handful of Manhattan blocks, it's full of people who care about this place, people who will do anything to save their town from being redeveloped into Anytown.

I love the way everyone has banded together for this cause, and the way Clara talks about it, her face flushed with passion, her eyes shining? Yeah, I'll admit, that's gone a long way in spurring me on to get involved in all the fundraising activities.

Sue me.

Asher, Weston, and Carson are already at the tent when I arrive, and I fist bump them all in greeting.

I eye their game day gear. "Did you all wear the thing I got for you under all that?"

"Yeah, but I'm not sure I'm in love with it, man," Weston says.

"Nah, it's just a bit of fun," Asher replies with a grin.

"I didn't get mine," Carson replies.

"I got you." I hand him a bag, and he pulls out one of the T-shirts I had printed for the event.

"You want me to wear this with a pair of swimming trunks?" Carson asks and I nod. "You do know I'm from the South. Ever heard of hypothermia, dude?"

"Crane's right. It's not exactly warm today," Weston adds.

I shrug. "Come on, guys. We're hockey players. We're the toughest of all the pros. What's a little cold to us?"

"I dunno. Those pickle ball guys are pretty fierce," a familiar voice says behind me, and I swing around to see Clara looking like a total babe-next-door with her blonde hair loose around her shoulders, and a cream pom-pom hat on top of her head. Her full, pillowy lips are pulled into a smile, her blue eyes sparkling.

"Pickle ball? Yeah, those guys sure are known for their brutal on-court fights," Asher replies, winning chortles from the other guys.

Me? I'm too busy staring at Clara to use actual words, because, heck, she looks so dang beautiful and just the sight of her is making my pulse leap.

"I got you a coffee," I say, passing her one of the cups.

"Thank you," she replies, and I ignore the looks the guys are throwing me.

"Hi, everyone," another voice says, and I refocus to see Keira at her side. "I'm Keira, Clara's sister."

"Hey," I reply as the other guys rumble their hellos.

"We're gonna head," Weston says, gesturing at the tent behind us. "Get ready for the drenching."

"Thanks again for doing this, guys," Clara says.

"Anything for the town," Carson replies, and then all three disappear into the tent.

"I think I mentioned to you that Keira runs the farmers' market," Clara explains.

I look around at the multiple vendors, forming a circle around a central bandstand where a three-piece band is playing. "You run all this?"

"It's not as complex as it looks, and besides, I grew up here, so I know every single one of the vendors," she replies.

"You're a couple of impressive sisters, you know that?" I say, meaning it.

The gorgeous sisters share a look, smiling.

"I don't know about that, but Keira sure is my angel," Clara says, giving Keira's arm a squeeze.

"Here's your coffee, honey," a deep voice says and I pull my gaze from Clara with the reluctance of a player sent to the penalty box to see a guy about my height, passing a coffee to Keira.

"You're Dan Roberts," I say as I extend my hand, more than a little starstruck. This guy was the captain of both the Ice Breakers charity team and the Chicago Blizzard and is one of the League's all-time top centers.

"Sure am, Cade Lennox," he replies, and yeah, that starstruck feeling doubles when it's clear he already knows who I am. "You guys should have had that Cup. The calls were garbage."

"Yeah, man. Total robbery by the zebras," I agree wholeheartedly, pumping Dan's hand.

"Zebras?" Clara questions.

Keira raises an index finger. "I know this one. That's the refs, because they wear black and white striped shirts."

"Your better half knows her stuff," I say to Dan, and Keira shrugs.

"You can't be married to a player-turned-coach without picking up some of the lingo," she says.

"How are you liking life here in Maple Falls?" Dan asks, and I glance at Clara, whose lips lift into that smile that makes my heart turn to jelly.

"It's spectacular," I reply, throwing Clara a wink.

She shakes her head, but she's still smiling.

Dan's eyes then dart between us, catching on in a millisecond. "Gotcha."

"I think what Cade is trying to say is that things are going well for him here, right, Cade?" Clara leads. "You're enjoying the team and the town, and you've got a great place to live."

"Yeah, that's exactly what I mean," I say with a grin.

"How did the filming of Cade's piano playing go?" Keira asks before she takes a sip of her coffee.

"We keep forgetting to do that, right, Cade?" Clara replies, and we share a smile.

"Hannah's learning piano. Did you know that?" Keira says.

"We spent some time at the keys together last night, actually," I reply.

Keira's brows lift. "Did you now?" She darts Clara a look, who quickly lifts her coffee cup to her lips and looks away.

Dan tilts his head at the Drench for Defense sign. "You doing this thing?"

"Sure am. Anything for this town I now call home," I reply. *And anything for Clara.* I don't say it. But I do definitely think it.

Man, I'm in deep with this girl. And I haven't even kissed her.

I make a mental note to remedy that as soon as possible.

"Speaking of which, you'd better get ready. We're due to start in ten minutes," Clara says.

"Catch you later when you're dripping wet," Dan says.

"I'm looking forward to it," I reply as I flash Clara a smile before I make my way into the tent, closing the entrance over.

Quickly, I get changed into my swimming trunks and the T-shirts I had monogrammed with *Ice Breakers Hockey: Saving Maple Falls One Splash at a Time.*

I had a special little nickname added for each of the guys, including for myself, and it'll be a fun surprise for Clara and everyone else when we don't waltz out of here in our game gear.

"Mama's Boy?" Weston asks, holding up his T-shirt with a look of distaste.

I shrug. "What dependable defenseman isn't a mama's boy?"

Weston laughs as he shakes his head before stripping down and throwing on the T.

"See? Totally suits you," I say. "Right, guys?"

Asher barks out a laugh. "You are *such* a mama's boy, Smith," he says.

"I'm not even gonna ask why I'm Cuddle Bear," Carson says, his tight features telling me he's not exactly thrilled with the name.

"Well, I'm happy," Asher declares, his arms out to the side as he does a turn, proudly showing off his Snuggle Muffin T.

"You're the cutest Snuggle Muffin I've ever seen," I tell him.

"You got that right," he replies, and we fist bump.

I slide my own T-shirt into place and Carson, Asher, and Weston all laugh, eyeing me.

"You are *so* a Cupcake," Asher says with a chortle.

I flash him my grin. "Loud and proud, baby. Loud and proud."

"You saved the worst one for yourself. Respect," Carson says.

"Whose is this?" Weston asks, pulling the final T-shirt from the bag. "It says Princess Sparkles."

"That'll be mine," says a voice from the tent entrance, and we turn to see our captain, Jamie Hayes, looking about as thrilled to be here as a rookie missing his first shot on goal.

"Yeah, it is!" I say as I pump the air with my fist. "Thanks for being here, Princess Sparkles. Me, Snuggle Muffin, Mama's Boy, and Cuddle Bear appreciate your service."

"Not exactly the way I like to spend my weekends, getting drenched in nothing but a T, but it's for a good cause, so I'm all in," Jamie replies as he takes the T-shirt from Weston, who couldn't wipe the smile from his face if he tried.

"Good to see ya, Princess Sparkles," Asher says with a grin, and wins a look from our captain.

Jamie arches a brow at me. "Why did you pick Princess Sparkles for me? Do I somehow give off princess vibes to you?"

"You sure do, Princess Sparkles. But you know what? It could have been worse," I say, gesturing at my own T-shirt. "And besides, a tough guy captain like you needs to get in touch with his feminine side every now and then, and what better way to do it than when you're being publicly drenched in water for charity?"

Jamie shakes his head, a smile teasing the edges of his mouth. "Not sure I have an eight-year-old girl feminine side in me."

He pulls on his T-shirt and I waggle my brows at him. "You do now."

"Are you guys decent?" Clara calls from behind the closed flap, and Jamie hurriedly pulls on his trunks.

"Of course we're not, but you can come in," Jamie replies. "We're a bunch of men wearing T-shirts that should probably have been given to a girl's birthday party." He throws me a meaningful look.

"All part of the fun," I assure him.

The door flap pulls open, and as Clara steps inside her eyes rove around the tent. "You guys look so pretty," she says, her lips quirking.

I do a little curtsy. "Thank you, miss."

"I thought you were going to wear your game day gear," she replies.

"We got a new plan, thanks to Lennox and his perplexing choice of nicknames for us all," Jamie replies.

She raises her brows. "You're responsible for these, Cade?"

"You're welcome," I say, my hands held out at my sides as I flash her my grin.

"Why does that not surprise me?"

"Because you know I'm awesome?" I tease.

"I guess it'll all be part of the fun. I thought our socials would go nuts for this in your game gear, and now?" She gestures at our chests. "Tell me, Cade, did you purposefully choose *white* T-shirts?"

"The team name looks best on white, just like our game day uniform," I go on to explain.

"You do know what happens to white T-shirts when they get wet, don't you?" she asks.

When white T-shirts get wet they…. Right. I didn't think of that.

"Lennox, you've made this event into some sort of a wet T-shirt competition!" Carson complains.

"Yeah, what's with that?" Jamie says.

"I suddenly feel so objectified," Asher adds, and I knit my

brows together as I look at him. "Nah, just kidding. It's all part of the fun, right?"

I push out a breath. "It's not like any of us are slouches in the body stakes. I'm okay with it if you guys are?"

They look among themselves.

"Yeah, we're good with it," Jamie says.

"In that case, we're ready to get this underway when you are," Clara says. "There's quite a crowd out there."

"We're ready," Jamie replies, and together, we follow her out of the tent, and a large crowd bursts into excited applause as we wave at them all.

A woman I recognize as Ashlyn, the mayor's daughter, is standing on the podium, a microphone in hand. Her brows ping up to meet her hairline as she takes in our T-shirts, and I wonder where the mayor is.

"Okay?" she mouths at Clara, who shrugs before she gives her the thumbs up.

"Ladies and gentlemen, boys and girls, welcome to the first ever Maple Falls Drench for Defense, with our new local hockey team, the Ice Breakers!" she exclaims, and as everyone cheers, we wave at the crowd.

She throws her eyes over us. "And I see the guys have got dressed up for the event today in *white* T-shirts with cute nicknames, which tells me this is going to be one for the ladies," Ashlyn continues, and there's an appreciative murmur among the womenfolk of the town.

"I hadn't thought about that angle," I call out, and it's clear either no one believes me or they simply do not care as they clap and cheer.

"If you haven't already bid on a bucket, you need to do so right now. We're closing bids in one minute," Ashlyn says and there's a rush.

I search the crowd for Clara and find her with her phone in hand, capturing everything going on. I lift my chin at her in acknowledgment, and she smiles back, her eyes soft. It does that weird thing in my chest again.

As I watch her as she chews on her lip, concentrating on getting the right angles for her videos, my heart tells me she's not only who I want in my life, but she's who I *need*, too.

All I've got to do now is tell her how I feel.

"First up, we have Carson Crane, whose usual nickname is Bama, but today he appears to be Cuddle Bear," Ashlyn announces.

Carson waves at the laughing and cheering crowd as he steps onto the drenching stage.

"Is your bucket of water ready, Dan?" Ashlyn asks. "Mr. Dan Roberts, everyone."

Dan Roberts steps forward, holding a bucket as the crowd cheers him on.

"We're ready when you are," Ashlyn says.

"This is for the town, Cuddle Bear," he says, and the crowd begins to chant "Cuddle Bear! Cuddle Bear! Cuddle Bear!" He chucks the bucket right at Carson, who lets out a surprised yelp as the water makes contact before he coughs and splutters as he takes in a mouthful, getting drenched from head to toe.

"And that's what we call a direct hit on Cuddle Bear, ladies and gentlemen!" Ashlyn declares as Carson wipes his eyes, giving a begrudging smile. His shirt has gone transparent but for the lettering and Ice Breakers logo, the damp fabric molded to his muscular torso, showing anyone who cares to look exactly how many muscles that guy has.

A bunch of people whistle and woot.

Yup, I have unwittingly turned this into a pervy wet T-shirt event.

"You're a good sport, Carson, and just by standing there and getting drenched you've already helped raise a lot of money for the town," Ashlyn says.

The crowd cheers and Carson gives a final wave before he steps back for the next victim.

"Next up we have Asher Tremblay, defenseman for the Ice Breakers, and if my eyes serve me right, today he's Snuggle Muffin. Is that right, Asher?" Ashlyn asks.

"Loud and proud," Asher replies with a grin before he breaks into a quick dance on the spot, showing the rest of us up and making the crowd go wild, clapping and cheering and calling out.

"We love you, Asher!" a woman calls from the crowd, and he acknowledges her with a wave. "Who's gonna drench this Snuggle Muffin?" he calls out, thrusting his thumbs at his chest.

A woman I don't recognize steps forward, bucket in hand, but I notice Asher seems to know exactly who she is by the way he squares his shoulder and throws her a flirty smile.

So, Asher's met a girl. He's kept that quiet.

"Go, Mabel!" a voice calls out, and the crowd begins to chant her name. Needing no further encouragement, Mabel steps forward and hurls the bucket's contents right over Asher.

He rallies, dripping wet, pumping his muscles in a total body builder pose.

"Another direct hit! Mabel McCluskey, you are on fire, girl!" Ashlyn says, and I put two and two together. Mabel must be Mary-Ellen McCluskey's daughter.

Mabel doesn't even crack a smile, instead simply throwing the crowd a look of triumph.

Huh. I wonder what her beef is with my man, Asher?

But I haven't got the time to ask as my name is called next.

"Cupcake, huh? That works," Ashlyn says with a laugh, and the crowd cheers. "Now we have right winger Cade Lennox stepping up to get drenched to save the town, sporting a T-shirt that declares we're to call him Cupcake from now on. Isn't that right, Cade?"

"Heck, yeah! I'm a total cupcake!" I say as I punch the air.

The crowd responds by chanting my new nickname. "Cupcake! Cupcake! Cupcake!"

I search for Clara, wondering—hoping—she'll be the one to

drench me. But instead, I spot her still filming, smiling as her sister, Keira, steps forward with Benny and Hannah. Hannah's holding the bucket, with a look of grim determination while her kid brother bounces around in obvious delight.

"Kids, how can you do this to me?" I ask, totally hamming it up, my arms splayed.

"Because you're called Cupcake *and* you play hockey!" Benny says in kid logic before he shrieks with laughter.

I throw my arms out to the side. "Hit me with your best shot, Hannah!"

But instead of Hannah, or even Benny, it's Keira who picks up the bucket, encouraged by her niece and nephew who are chanting "Cupcake! Cupcake! Cupcake!" along with the rest of the crowd.

I glance at Clara. She's still filming, and she's watching me with a quiet gaze, a smile quirking her lips. Man, I would do anything to have her look at me like that all day long, including getting drenched by her sister—which is about to happen right now.

As Keira lifts the bucket, ready to douse me, I hold Clara's gaze, my heart telling me she's the one for me, and even though I'm expecting it, the slap of the cold water against my torso, across my face, and running down my legs is a total shock.

But the cheer of the crowd and the chanting of "Cupcake! Cupcake! Cupcake!" helps me through it, and when I grin out at the crowd, I notice Clara's eyes are still trained on me, that smile momentarily peppered with concern, before her lips pull up into the biggest and best smile I've seen all day.

With my T-shirt clinging to my body, I throw out a couple of poses and the crowd goes wild.

Next, Weston gets drenched by a woman called Fiona while the crowd chants for "Mama's Boy" to a frenzied pitch. He takes it all in his stride, waving and smiling out at the crowd.

Finally, it's the captain's turn, Jamie Hayes, aka Princess Sparkles, who gets a huge cheer as Ashlyn temporarily hands over her MC duties, obviously relishing throwing her bucket of water over the guy.

I need to remember to ask my friend about what's going on there later.

And then all of us hockey players line up, our shirts clinging to every muscle to whistles and hoots from the crowd, and I throw Clara a wink as we pose and ham it up to the tune "It's Raining Men," the crowd loving every single moment.

As the adrenaline from being drenched wears off and the cold begins to seep into my bones, I'm grateful when Mrs. McCluskey passes me a towel as we return to the tent to get changed.

"Is Mabel your daughter, the one who drenched Asher?" I ask.

"She is," she says, beaming at me. "You've got a thing for Clara Johnson, huh?" she asks in my ear, her eyes twinkling.

"What makes you say that?"

"Oh, I notice things," she replies with a smirk. "Shared looks, the way your eyes always find her. And you, young man, have quite the reputation with the ladies." I open my mouth to defend myself but don't get the chance when she adds, "You take care of Clara's heart, now. That girl has been through enough."

"Yes, ma'am," I reply.

Mrs. McCluskey's words stick with me as I towel off in the tent and change back into my clothes from earlier. She's right, I do watch Clara constantly. The way she laughed when Carson yelped as the cold water hit him, how she grinned when Asher struck a dramatic pose, the way she was momentarily concerned for me after my drenching until she saw I was okay. The genuine joy on her face as she captured every ridiculous but fun moment of the event.

Clara has been guarded with me, and for good reason. But what she doesn't know is that somewhere between her resistance and me watching her fierce love for Hannah and Benny, I stopped being the guy who never gets serious with a woman.

This is about me wanting to be the man who earns the right to be a part of her world. The man who gets to make her laugh until she snorts, who gets to kiss away the worry lines that appear when she's stressed. To rub her feet when she's tired at the end of a long day.

I've spent most of my adult life purposefully and successfully avoiding exactly this kind of complication. But I'm not avoiding it anymore.

I'm running straight toward it.

CHAPTER 15
CLARA

MY HEAD IS full of Cade. The way he stepped up to do the Drench for Defense without a second thought, for me and for the town. The self-deprecating T-shirts he had made for himself and the other guys, poking fun at their tough guy hockey personas and making the town laugh. The softness in his gaze as he looked at me before my sister stepped forward to douse him with water.

And yes, the way he looked in his wet T-shirt, all muscular and strong, his confident smile never wavering.

I pull out my phone and tap out a message to Bailey.

ME:

I've made a decision.

BAILEY:

Is this about your complicated love triangle?

ME:

I'm breaking things off with Warrior. He's been great, but I want real. I want now. And somehow, real and now look a whole lot like someone else.

My phone begins to ring in my hand and I press "answer."

"Who are you and what have you done with my cautious friend?" Bailey asks.

"I guess I got beyond liking him from a distance. I know this may sound corny, but it's true. Cade makes me feel seen for the first time in years."

"You're falling for him?"

"I don't know how we'll make it work, but I want to at least try. I'm tired of being scared of everything going wrong, Bailey. What if it actually goes right?"

"And the non-fraternization clause?"

"I'll deal with that," I say, sounding a hundred times more confident than I feel.

"Then you, my dear, will have one heck of a story to tell. Now go get your man."

I feel giddy at the thought. "I need to tell Warrior first."

"That's the right thing to do. Good luck. Love you loads."

"Love you loads, too."

I lean back against my sofa, warmth and calmness spreading across my chest and wrapping me up in an embrace. Falling for Cade Lennox is the gift I never knew I needed, and now that I know how I feel about him with total clarity, there are some things I've got to do before I can take things with him to the next level.

I pull up the app on my phone and go to my most recent chat with Warrior. I read the last message from him, guilt worming its way across my chest. "You have come to mean so much to me," I read. "I can't imagine having gone through this without you."

I take a breath, my thumbs poised over the keyboard. I know what I have to do. I know I'm about to hurt Warrior. But my conscience won't allow me not to do this. I'm falling for another man, and Warrior deserves the truth from me. I tap out a one-word message.

ME:

Hi

I stare at the screen, my insides in knots, waiting.

CHRONICWARRIOR88:

I'm so happy to hear from you. It's been days! Are you okay? Have you had a relapse? Please say you haven't.

That worm of guilt coils its way around through me and tightens its grip.

ME:

I'm fine. You're so sweet to ask. But I do need to tell you something, and in truth, I've been putting it off like a coward. It's time to step up.

CHRONICWARRIOR88:

What is it? You know you can tell me anything.

I tap out the words I know I need to say. *You have been such an important part of my life these past few months, and I'm so glad that I've met you. But the fact of the matter is I'm falling for another man, and I thought you should know.*

I'm about to press send when another message pops up on my screen.

I'm in Maple Falls and I thought I would come by and surprise you.

Wait, what? My heart leaps into my mouth. Warrior's in Maple Falls?

CHRONICWARRIOR88:

Can we meet?

I chew on my lip, my mind whirring. Meeting him to end things would be the right thing to do. In fact, it's probably the only thing to do now.

ME:

Let's meet at Shirley May's Diner in thirty minutes. It's on Main Street.

There's a knock on the door, making me jerk back from my phone.

"I'll get it!" Benny yells from down the hall, and I click my phone off and follow him.

Benny pulls the door open to reveal his dad, standing on the doorstep, flowers in hand. He stands there like no time has passed with the same smug half-smile, wearing the same jacket I used to steal when I was cold.

My heart doesn't flutter anymore at the sight of my ex-husband. It hasn't for a long time. Rather, it clenches, my jaw tightening.

"Daddy!" Benny calls out as he leaps into his father's arms.

"Woah!" Dwayne responds, balancing the flowers and his son.

I pull my brows together in confusion. "Dwayne, what are you doing here? It's not your weekend."

He plants a kiss on Benny's check and then sets him on the floor. "These are for you," he says, thrusting the flowers at me.

More out of reflex than anything, I take them.

"They're your favorite," he tells me.

I look down at the bunch of white roses. They were never my favorite, but Dwayne never bothered to learn that.

I don't point it out. There's no point in being petty.

"Thank you," I say through tight lips.

Hannah darts into the hallway and immediately throws herself at her father. "Daddy!"

"How are you, sweetheart?" Dwayne plants a kiss on Hannah's cheek.

"What are you doing here, Dwayne?" I repeat.

"I was in town for work and stayed over last night. Hey, I caught the Drench for Defense thing. You were filming for your new job, right?"

"That's right."

"Anyway, I thought I'd pop by to see my favorite people."

His favorite people? Didn't he give up that position when he walked out on us all those years ago?

Dwayne produces a lollipop for each of our kids, and they grab them gleefully.

"Thanks, Daddy," they both say.

"Why don't you two go to the playroom and I'll be down there soon? I need to talk with your mommy first."

The kids take off excitedly, dropping the lollipop wrappers on the floor, leaving the two of us in the hallway. I pick up the wrappers and turn and walk into the living room, where I offer him a seat, placing the white roses on the coffee table.

"What is it, Dwayne?" I ask without preamble.

"Come on, Clars," he says, using his old nickname for me. "We're both adults. We can talk amicably, can't we?"

I force the tension in my shoulders to ease. "Of course. Sorry. I was in the middle of something when you got here and I wasn't expecting you. That's all."

His lips lift into the smile I once fell for when I was a naïve nineteen-year-old, away from home at college, his confidence and good looks pulling me in from the moment I laid eyes on him.

To my surprise, he reaches for my hand. "May I?"

"You want to hold hands with me?" I ask, incredulous. This is the man who's barely spoken a civil word to me for years, the man who only turns up every month or two to see his kids, despite the divorce agreement that allowed him a weekend every fortnight.

"Is that so wrong? You're the mother of my children, Clars, the woman I should never have left."

I blink at him in shock. "What did you just say?" I ask, my voice like a thin reed.

He collects my hand in his. "Look. I made mistakes when you got sick. I was scared, and I didn't know how to help you. But I've grown, I've changed."

I look down at my hand in his like it's not a part of me, totally disassociated from the rest of my body.

"I need to tell you something," he continues.

Warily, I look back at him. "I'm still dealing with the first thing you said, Dwayne."

"Look, I knew if I reached out as me, you'd never give me a chance. But we connected so well once more. That was the real us, without all the baggage."

Connected so well once more? What the heck is he talking about?

"Dwayne, you're not making any sense."

His smile spreads, the look in his eyes telling me he's in on some great secret he has yet to share.

"Can we sit?" he asks, and I nod, immediately pulling my hand from his and taking a seat on one of the sofas.

I fully expect him to sit opposite me, but instead he lowers himself onto the seat cushion beside me, our thighs merely inches apart.

I swallow, my back stiffening. "You're acting weird. What's going on?" I demand.

"May I?" he asks, holding out his hand once more.

I give a tight head shake, pressing my lips together.

"Tell me about Warrior."

I recoil from him in shock, my pulse jumping. "How do you know about Warrior?"

That grin of his doesn't falter for a second. "As I said, I knew if I reached out to you as me, you'd never have given me a chance. But as Warrior, you opened up. You let me back in."

My jaw slackens as my mind races faster than a Formula 1 race car. Dwayne is Warrior? Warrior is Dwayne? My ex-husband has been masquerading as someone with CFS, someone who I formed what I had thought was a close, genuine relationship with online?

I blink at him in utter shock. "You're Warrior?" Dismay shortens my breath as I scramble to align the radically different people in my mind. Dwayne, my ex-husband, who cheated on me with someone **who I thought was my friend**, and then left me and the kids. A man who barrels through life, never thinking of anyone but himself. And Warrior, the sweet, thoughtful man with chronic fatigue, who brought a sense of calm to my world, giving me an outlet, both of us mutually supportive.

Only it was all a lie.

Dwayne doesn't have CFS. Dwayne isn't a sweet and tender person who brings a sense of calm to my life.

Those two people could not be more different.

"I know this is a lot to take, but can't you see what this means? You and me, Clars. We're meant to be together, our connection online these past months is all the proof we needed. You didn't even know it was me and you fell for me, all over again."

He scoots closer, placing a hand on my shoulder. "It's over with Izzy, Clars. Done with. I left her. And it's because of you. You and me? We're made for each other. Can't you see that?"

Thoughts are still flying around in my head like I'm taking corners at 200 mph with no brakes as I wrangle with understanding the depth of his concealment, his manipulation, his sheer gall.

Finally, I find my voice.

"Dwayne, please get your hand off of me," I say levelly, my jaw tight, my body as rigid as a plank of wood.

He doesn't remove it. "Hey, I know I wasn't a hundred percent honest online, and I'm sorry about that. But you locked me out, Clars. I couldn't get you to see sense. I needed to get through to you, and I knew you wouldn't let Dwayne back in."

I gawk at him. "I can't believe you did this to me."

"Can't you see how *romantic* this is? It's next level romantic, babe. Warrior was my only option to show you that whatever has gone before, whatever mistakes we both made—and we did both make mistakes, babe—," He looks at me pointedly, as though I had some part in what happened back then, as if me getting sick was somehow my mistake, and that I'm equally to blame for him leaving me for a woman I once counted as a friend. "You can't fight it, babe. You and me? We're meant to be."

Finally, he falls into silence.

"I said, get your hand off of me," I grind out, my tone low and firm.

He holds both hands in the air. "Okay. You win."

I stare at him. "*Win*? You think this is me *winning*?" I spring to my feet, suck in a breath, and square my shoulders, anger rushing through my veins. I look down at him. "You think that manipulating me through Warrior is just a means to an end? A way to work your way back into my affections?"

"Babe, come on. I had to do it. I had no choice. You barely even talk to me when I come to pick up the kids."

I force myself to remain calm. The kids are only just down the hall, and I need to get my message through to him without alarming them. "You didn't. If you wanted to work on our relationship, you should have done it honestly. Not by creating some fiction with which to lure me in."

He rises to his feet. "But you fell for Warrior. You fell for *me*."

I shake my head, a bitter laugh bubbling out of me. "I was going online to end things with him just now."

His features drop momentarily before he pulls them back into a smile. "No, you weren't. You're just saying that to make yourself look better. But babe, you don't need to worry about that. I'm here, and I want you back."

"Stop. Just stop talking." I suck in air, my heart hammering. "What you did wasn't romantic. It was manipulation. You took my genuine concern for someone on the same health journey as me, hiding behind it like a coward."

"Babe—"

I raise my hand to stop any more diatribe from spilling from his mouth.

I've had enough.

"After you left, it took me a long time to trust again. I trusted Warrior, but it was a lie. Do you have any idea how that makes me feel?"

"But you can trust me. I'm Warrior. Warrior is me."

I cross my arms and glare at him, my resolve strengthening with every fast beat of my heart. "You don't get to waltz back into my life through deception."

"You're making a bigger deal of that part than you should. It was a means to an end. That's all."

"And the fact that you don't see what you did? That's enough to tell me that I could never be with you again, let alone all the other stuff. I've built a good life for myself and our kids, and I've done it on my own. And now?" My throat heats, and I fight to control the tears threatening my eyes. "Now I'm falling for someone else, someone who accepts me as me, all of me. He sees my chronic fatigue as a part of me, not something to run from."

His whole demeanor turns stormy. "What? Who is this guy?"

I ignore his question. Cade has nothing to do with how I feel about Dwayne and the way he's treated me.

Instead, I press on with what I want to say. "We're done, you and me. We were done the day you left. You will always be

Hannah and Benny's father, and I can only hope you can find it in yourself to take that role more seriously than you have in the past. Now, I want you to leave."

"You're making a mistake. No one can give you what I gave you."

"You're right," I say, and watch as his features lift in momentary optimism. "No one can give me the level of heartache and abandonment that you did. No one." I move past him, heading toward the door, which I pull open, allowing the cold in. "I'll see you next weekend when you come to pick the kids up," I say firmly.

"This isn't over," he grinds out before he steps out onto the stoop.

"That's where you're wrong, Dwayne. This is over." And with a deep level of satisfaction, I swing the door closed on him, both literally and metaphorically, before I lock it and lean back against it, my heart hammering against my ribs like it's trying to escape my chest.

The wood is solid and reassuring against my spine—much like my newfound backbone.

Who knew I had it in me? All these years, I thought confrontation was my kryptonite, it turns out, I just needed the right kind of righteous fury to discover I've got a spine made of pure titanium. The irony isn't lost on me that Dwayne just got schooled by the woman he once convinced she was too weak to handle real life. The same woman who used to apologize for having chronic fatigue, as if getting sick was some personal failing that required constant penance.

I push myself off the door and walk slowly to the living room window. I watch Dwayne's retreating figure disappear down the path and into his car, his tires squealing as he beats a hasty retreat. He's probably going to spend the next hour trying to figure out what went wrong with his grand romantic gesture. And I guess he's about to discover that catfishing your ex-wife isn't exactly the love story women dream of.

"Mommy?" Hannah's voice pulls me from my thoughts. "Is Daddy coming back?"

Suddenly exhausted, I turn toward my daughter. "Maybe next weekend, sweetheart. But you know what?"

"What?"

"We're going to be just fine."

And the beautiful thing is, I know it to be true.

CHAPTER 16
CADE

"GOOD WORK TODAY, MEN," Coach says as we catch our breath after another grueling practice. "As you know, our first game is next week against the Great Lake Vikings, and we need to be ready. Simpson," he says with the faintest hint of a grin. "That lacrosse move you pulled was impressive as heck, but save the highlight reel stuff for when we're up by five goals, got that?"

Nate shrugs. "Come on, Coach, you've gotta admit that last slapshot was a thing of beauty."

"It was reckless and selfish. That fancy stuff stays in your back pocket until we've got a comfortable lead. You pull moves like that when the game's on the line, and you'll be watching the rest of it from the bench."

"Come on, it was awesome," he persists, and several of the team scoff.

Coach shoots him a look that could wither at fifty paces. "Pull your head in, son. And do it before next week's game. Got it?"

"Yes, Coach," he replies, although I know what he's thinking because I've been there myself when I was young and had a lot to prove. You want to make your name, and you think you're invincible.

But Nate doesn't have the rookie excuse. He's got enough ice time under his belt to read the room. I guess some players just don't get there's no *I* in *team*, no matter how long they've been playing.

"Captain, any words?" Coach asks, and Jamie glides over to us.

"Good effort out there today, but we've got some things to clean up before our first game, as Coach says. Bama, that shot selection in the third drill was money. Keep trusting your instincts in tight spaces."

"Will do," Carson replies.

"Smith, your positioning on that two-on-one was textbook, but you hesitated on the clear. Don't think so much, just move the puck."

"You got it," Weston replies.

"And Simpson? Coach is right. Pull your head in and be part of the team."

Nate doesn't reply. He just gives a half smile that tells me he has no intention of pulling his head in any time soon.

Jamie scans the group, making eye contact with each of us. "We're building something special here in Maple Falls, but it starts with showing up for each other every single day. That's how we earn not only our position in the League, but this town's respect."

"You got it, Captain!" I say along with a bunch of the guys.

"Excuse me?" a woman says, and I turn, expecting to see Clara. She's expected here to film a few of us who volunteered to do another dance—me, of course, and Asher, the shoo-in, but also Clément and Carson this time. But it isn't Clara. It's a young woman, looking nervous, clasping a phone in her hand, dwarfed by a puffer jacket that reaches below her knees.

"What can I do for you, miss?" Coach asks.

"I'm here to film the dance?" She poses it as a question although it's clearly not one. "I'm Millie. Millie Nelson. I work in the marketing team."

"Where's Clara?" I ask, and there's a murmur among the guys.

"Missing your girlfriend?" Nate jibes.

"Whatever," I reply with a roll of my eyes.

"Clara's sick today, so I'm here instead," Millie says, looking like a nervous rookie who just got called up to face a charging defenseman.

I pull my brows together. Clara's sick? That can't be good. I hope it's not a CFS flare.

"I've got a list of players who I'll be filming, if you could please stay behind? Asher Tremblay, Carson Crane, Cade Lennox, and Clément Rivière," she says, pronouncing Clément's name as Clément Rivi-ear.

"You've got your instructions. The rest of you, hit the showers. And you need to really bring it at our next practice!" Coach says as the team begins to peel off.

Instead of hanging around, I tell Millie that I'm sorry I can't film today, and I dash to the locker room to get showered and changed at lightning speed.

A short while later, I've got a bunch of fruit and some chicken soup, and I arrive at Clara's house, and knock on the door.

"Who is it?" I hear Clara call out.

"It's me, Cade."

The door opens enough so I can see Clara in a pale T-shirt and pair of black leggings, her pretty blonde hair captured in a messy bun on top of her head, and a plaid blanket thrown around her shoulders. The sight of her looking so vulnerable squeezes my heart, and I have the urge to collect her in my arms and carry her to her bed, then lay down beside her and hold her close, protecting her from whatever it is that's made her unwell.

"Hey," she says, rubbing her eyes.

"I heard you were sick, so I thought I'd bring you some supplies."

Her features lift into a smile. "That's so sweet of you. I'm not contagious, if you want to come in? But I warn you, the place is a mess."

Wild horses could not stop me.

A moment later, we're in her living room, a homey place with a wooden fireplace, comfy sofas, and evidence of kids all around, with pictures on the walls, a toy box under the window, and Benny's hockey stick lying on a sofa.

Clara immediately starts to plump cushions, and as I reach out and place my hand on her shoulder it strikes me that I'm falling for a woman I've barely even touched, let alone kissed.

The old Cade would be looking at me like I was crazy right about now.

But the old me is gone. Buried. The new me is confident in his feelings for this woman here with me, and I know deep in my heart that she's the one I want to be with.

"Stop. There's no need to clean up on my account," I say softly.

"But you've never been here before," she protests.

"I'm not here for the décor, Triple. Sit. Put your feet up."

She does as I instruct, and I sit beside her, pulling her feet to rest in my lap.

"What's wrong? Is it a CFS flair?" I ask gently, my hand on her sock-clad feet.

"I think so. I woke up today feeling like my body was shot-full of lead. I didn't want to have to call in sick, but I needed to take the day."

"Dr. Bernice would be proud. You're managing your energy levels."

"And Owen would be relieved I'm not superhuman after all."

"You're pretty dang superhuman to me," I say, and her lips lift into a small smile.

"I'm not sure there are all that many superheroes whose strength is being a mom to a couple of kids and trying to hold down a full-time job."

"There should be. What brought this on? Have you been working too hard?"

"A little," she replies, and she says it in such a way that makes me wonder if she's holding something back.

"Is that all?"

She twists her mouth as she plays with her hands.

"You don't have to tell me. I'm just concerned, that's all."

"No, I want to. I just needed some time to process it."

"Is me heating up some chicken soup for you long enough?" I ask, only half joking.

"I think that should do it. But I can manage to heat some soup up. Thanks for bringing it." She goes to move.

"Stay. Just tell me where the kitchen is and I'll get this bad boy heated."

"You sure?"

"Positive."

A few minutes later, I have heated up the soup, found a tray, a spoon, and a napkin, and placed it on the coffee table in front of Clara.

"You're such a thoughtful person," she says as I resume my position at her side.

"Give the people what they want, that's what I always say."

She smiles, her eyes brighter than they were only a few

moments ago. "I think I'm just tired out, that's all. I don't have that crushing fatigue I've suffered with in the past."

I settle back onto the sofa, lifting her feet onto my lap once more. "That's good to hear. Tired out we can deal with, right?"

"I also know what brought this on. My ex turned up yesterday."

"Was it his turn for the kids?"

"No. He wanted to talk with me." She pulls her lips into a line. "He told me he wants me back."

My whole body stills. "He wants you back?" I repeat as my throat tightens, thoughts pinging around my brain like balls in a pinball machine.

He's the kids' dad.

Clara was in love with him before.

She leans forward and places her hand on my arm. "Cade, I told him I was done."

Relief floods my veins and my face breaks into a grin. "You had me worried there for a sec, Triple."

She shakes her head. "Trust me, there's nothing to worry about. I am well and truly over him, and what's more, he showed his true colors yesterday."

I narrow my eyes, my body tensing. "He didn't hurt you, did he? Because if he did—"

"No. Nothing like that. It turns out, he'd been manipulating me, pretending to be someone else online, someone with whom I had become close."

A sharp tension coils within me. She's close to someone online? A man? A man who was in fact her ex?

I'm not quite sure how to feel right now.

"But it was a lie. He'd tried to catfish me to prove that we were meant to be together."

My jaw clenches as my blood heats in my veins. "He did *what*?" I grind out through clenched teeth.

"He pretended to be a man with CFS, someone who needed me to support him on his journey." She looks down at her hands.

"At one point, I thought I had feelings for Warrior—that was the name he used. But that was before…? Well, that was before I met you." As she lifts her gaze to mine once more, I see the sincerity in her big blue eyes, and all the tension, the anger I felt only seconds ago, drains right out of me.

Her features lift into the most beautiful smile, and I know that my time has finally come.

I'm going to tell her how much she means to me.

"Clara," I begin, my voice hoarse. I shift closer to her, her knees now in my lap. Resting a hand on them, I look into her eyes and say, "I'm totally out of my depth with you."

She swallows hard, and I can see something shift in her expression as she gazes back at me. "You are?" she asks, and there's a note of such vulnerability in her voice that it nearly undoes me completely.

Here I am, a guy who's made a career out of reading plays before they develop, of never getting in deep with anyone, and I can't even figure out how to tell this woman that she's completely changed my way of thinking, my way of life.

That it's her I want, and her alone.

"The old me wasn't looking for anything real. I was young and living the carefree, single life. You heard the stories. But I grew tired of it, of never having anything real with anyone. When the opportunity to come to Maple Falls presented itself, I jumped at it as a chance to start afresh, to reinvent myself," I tell her.

The words are coming easier now, like I've finally found the right play to call. "Now? I'm older. Wiser. Hopefully." I can't help but smile at that last part, because let's be honest, wisdom is still a work in progress where I'm concerned. "I hoped over time I might meet someone, someone to laugh with, to connect with, to get deep with." I take a breath before I say what I've wanted to say for some time, ever since I first began to feel it. "Clara. Triple. I've found that in you. As short as it's been since we met, I'm falling in love with you. *Am* in love with you."

There it is. The words I've been carrying around like a puck I couldn't quite get a clean shot on. Out there in the open.

My heart is hammering, my insides doing a triple axel worthy of Olympic gold

Does she feel it too?

Sure, I know she's attracted to me. But this goes way beyond that. This is soul deep, like the rocks buried deep within the earth, and finally giving voice to how I feel has me both elated and vulnerable in a way I've never experienced before.

Her eyes widen, and for a heartbreaking split second I wonder if I've just made the biggest mistake of my life.

But then she speaks, and her voice is soft and breathless and everything I didn't know I needed to hear. "I'm in love with you, too, Cade."

And that's it. Game *over*.

This is Clara finally letting me in, letting her walls down for me, and it's a thing of beauty.

I reach up and push a stray hair from her cheek, the brush of my fingertips against her soft skin sending electricity coursing down my spine. "You are?"

"Cade," she murmurs, and the emotion she puts into saying my name spurs me on to cup her chin in my hands, marveling at how small and perfect she feels, her skin soft. I lean over to her, and when I brush my lips against hers, it's the most tender, heartfelt kiss of my life, full of love and longing for this incredible woman.

She shifts her body closer to me, her hands sliding up my neck and tangling in my hair, and we deepen our kiss as every look, every smile, every second we've shared since the day we met melds together to form this very moment, both of us laid bare, showing what we mean to one another.

Her lips are soft, her taste incredible, and I never want this moment to end. Just her and me, locked together in the strength of our shared love for one another.

When finally I pull away, she's looking at me like I've just scored the game-winning goal in overtime. "That was nice."

"Nice?" I repeat with a chuckle. "I think it was more than nice." I brush my lips against hers once more to prove my point, and feel her tremble in my arms. "Do you know I've wanted to kiss you since the moment I laid eyes on you," I murmur into her hair.

"You mean when you called me 'ma'am?'" she teases, and there's that wit I've fallen for, sharp and perfectly timed, even when she's looking at me like she wants to pull me back down for another kiss.

"Would you forgive me if I kissed you again?" I ask, already knowing the answer but wanting to hear the words from her lips.

"Only if you kiss me like you really, really mean it," she replies and my laugh rumbles up from somewhere deep in my chest as I scoop her up onto my lap, pulling her small frame against me and tangling my fingers in her hair.

She closes her eyes and lets out a little whimper. It spurs me on to claim her mouth with mine once more, this time with less tentativeness. This time with less reserve. I kiss her hard and long, and every coherent thought I've ever had flies right out the window.

Because this perfect kiss with Clara Johnson is the only play that matters anymore.

CHAPTER 17
CLARA

MY HEART IS FULL, I'm wearing the hugest grin, and not even the cold, driving Pacific Northwest rain can dent my happiness as I dash down the street to Maple Grounds on Main Street. I push through the door and am immediately hit by the smell of fresh coffee, pumpkin, and cinnamon in the air, the warmth winding its way around me as I lower my hood.

I'm in love with Cade Lennox.

I'm in love with *Cade Lennox*.

Oh, my, I still can't get used to that.

But it's the truth. I fell in love with the last man on earth I ever thought would be right for me, and it turns out he's the most wonderful of men—and everything that's been missing in my life.

Loving him is like finding myself in a place that feels like home, a deep sense of calm and happiness filling my chest and radiating out into the world.

Cade Lennox is so much more than I ever thought he would be, and loving him is the greatest gift of my life.

I let out a contented sigh.

If the me from summer could see this version of me in fall, she would fully expect I'd either had a personality transplant or somehow lost the ability to think rational thoughts. In my Clara summer philosophy, guys like Cade were to be treated with extreme caution, rebuffing any flirty talk thrown my way, my approach less *heart on my sleeve* and a whole lot more *heart locked away safely in a panic room with a backup generator.*

And now the walls of that panic room have been well and truly knocked down in the most wonderful of ways, and I've allowed myself to trust again. To love again.

You know what? There's something about being in love that makes absolutely everything better, like you're wearing the biggest pair of rose-tinted glasses and nothing can permeate them.

Benny and Hannah fighting at breakfast over who got the last bowl of cereal and who had to settle for toast? No problem.

The fact I couldn't find a parking space outside the bakery and had to park around the corner and dash down the street through the wind and the rain? It's like a soft summer breeze, playfully teasing my hair.

After we shared our feelings with one another, Cade stayed with me for the rest of the day, snuggled up beside me on the sofa, talking and kissing and kissing some more. He wouldn't let me lift a finger to do anything, insisting I relax and recharge, caring for me in a way Dwayne never could.

Cade was there to greet the kids when they came home from school, making them snacks and listening to their stories from their days alongside me. He helped Hannah practice the piano on our rickety old upright, telling us Bess would be jealous but that he'd give her a polish to make up for it when he got home. It made Hannah giggle so hard she almost fell off the piano stool.

He spent a long time talking with Benny about hockey and their favorite topic, *The Timekeeper Chronicles*. When he saw that Benny had ripped open the packaging of the collectible Cade had given him, I caught the flash of pain that crossed Cade's face —but to his credit, it didn't faze him enough to say anything, and he played make believe with Benny, both of them in their comic book world.

Then, when evening came, I insisted I was well enough to cook dinner, and after much debate, he agreed to help me, and we worked side by side in my kitchen, preparing a meal of mac and cheese as the kids played.

It was like we were a brand-new family, and I'm not going to deny how amazing it felt.

The next day, my energy had improved but not enough to spend an entire day at work on top of my mom duties, so I agreed with Veronica I would work the mornings only for the next couple days and review things on Friday.

Which brings me today, the day I'm back at work full time for the first time this week, my energy steady, ready to deal with what comes next, aka the non-fraternization clause in my employment contract.

Cade and I may have become a couple as of Monday morning—four blissful days ago—and we've definitely spent as much time together as was humanly possible in that time, but we've not shared our newfound love with anyone else yet. Not even with Keira and Dan, and as far as the kids know, Cade is just the friendly hockey player he's always been, and nothing more.

Now, I need to come clean to Veronica about this new relationship and hope like heck she can see how genuine we are about one another. Hence the dash into Maple Grounds to get her a coffee and one of the bakery's fall-themed pumpkin cinnamon rolls that is always a delicious, sweet treat.

"You look like one of those drowned otters down by the creek, Clara Johnson," Mary-Ellen McCluskey says from her table by the window. "Doesn't she look like a drowned otter, Suzette?"

Great. The town gossip and one of her minions. Just what I need.

Suzette Donnelly looks me up and down. "She does, Mary-Ellen, only one who seems quite happy about the situation."

"Do I?" I reply with the same smile I've not been able to wipe off my face since Monday morning at approximately 9:47 a.m., aka the moment Cade turned up at my house with concern furrowing his brow.

Not that I'm counting.

Oh, who am I kidding? I'm counting every minute of being in love.

Both Mary-Ellen McCluskey and Suzette Donnelly shoot me a look as though I've quite clearly lost my mind. And you know what? They may well be right. Didn't someone once say that love is a temporary insanity?

"We were just talking about the Drench for Defense at the weekend. What a wonderful event," Mary-Ellen says.

"And what a handsome group of hockey players in their wet shirts, too," Suzette adds, her eyes dancing.

"We agreed it was for a good cause, even if it straddled the line of good taste, you understand," Mary-Ellen adds, referring to the whole wet T-shirt situation. "Come and sit with us, Clara. You can answer a burning question for us."

"I need to grab a couple coffees to go actually, Mrs. McCluskey," I tell her.

"You go do that, and we'll keep this seat nice and warm for you for when you get back." She pats the seat between her and Suzette, shooting me a knowing smile.

"You got it," I reply, hoping I can slip out undetected before she gets me in her grasp, shining the sharp light of interrogation in my eyes.

But then she wouldn't be the Queen of Maple Falls Gossip if she didn't manage to prize information out of people on the regular.

I make my way to the counter where I order a couple of take-out coffees and the pumpkin cinnamon roll for Veronica from Lola, one of my high school English teacher's daughters who's about twenty-one or twenty-two.

"On behalf of the female population of this town, I want to thank you for the Drench for Defense, Clara," she tells me as she slots the pumpkin cinnamon roll into a paper bag with a pair of tongs. "Not only did me and my friends catch the live event, but we've been watching the videos you posted, too."

"I'm glad you enjoyed it."

"Those guys are all so freaking hot, don't you think? All those muscles upon muscles," she says in a low voice as though she might get in trouble over expressing the opinion. "I never knew someone could have that many. How did we ever get so lucky to get our own NHL team here in Maple Falls?"

My belly does a little flip as my mind instantly turns to Cade. Although I agree with Lola that he and the rest of the guys looked hot in their wet T-shirts, absolutely nothing beats the look in Cade's eyes when he smiles at me, so full of love and tenderness and heart.

Not even all those "muscles upon muscles."

"We are lucky, especially as the team is doing what they can to help save the town," I reply.

"I guess you'll be at the inaugural bash on Saturday, since you work for the team," she says. "I wish I could go, but there's not a lot of call for a barista on the team. Hey, unless there *is* a call for a barista on the team?" She looks at me hopefully.

"I'll let you know if things change and a barista gets added to the team list," I reply with a laugh.

Her eyes dance. "That would be the best job *ever*."

She makes the coffee, and with the paper bag containing the pumpkin cinnamon roll dangling from my fingers and with cups in hand, I'm hoping to sidle past the gossipmongers and escape their interrogation.

But I didn't factor in the extreme commitment Mary-Ellen McCluskey has to her craft, even going to the point where she stands up and blocks the doorway so that I can't make my escape.

"Come, Clara. Sit." Her tone is uncompromising, and so I do as she says, despite every bone in my body screaming at me to *abort! abort! abort!*

"I've only got a minute," I warn as I lower myself onto the seat. "I need to get this coffee to my boss."

"We'll make it snappy, won't we, Suzette?" she says.

"Always," Suzette replies.

Mary-Ellen clasps her hands, her elbows resting on the table as she pins me with her gaze. "You know, I've been meaning to ask you about that handsome young man who's been spending so much time at your house lately."

I could play dumb, but the fact of the matter is Mary-Ellen McCluskey lives right across the street from me. The chances she would have seen Cade's black BMW SUV are pretty high.

"Cade's helping Hannah with piano," I say, which is, of course, strictly speaking, true. It's just not the whole picture.

She and Suzette share a look.

"Piano lessons, you say?" Mary-Ellen nods sagely, as if this explains everything. "And does he always bring dinner to these piano lessons? Because Mildred Henderson saw him carrying a casserole dish to your front door Tuesday evening, and frankly, dear, I've never known piano teachers to provide dinner. Have you, Suzette?"

Suzette shakes her head. "No, Mary-Ellen. I've not."

"Cade's very thorough in his teaching methods, and he insisted on feeding everyone to help keep Hannah's energy up,"

I reply with the world's weakest argument, my cheeks beginning to heat.

Mary-Ellen's eyes sparkle with glee. "Oh, I'm sure he is very thorough. Very *hands-on*, I imagine."

Oh, the innuendo. Mrs. McCluskey could give Cade explaining the finer details of hockey a run for his money.

"Especially when it comes to proper finger placement," Suzette adds. "On the piano keys, of course."

"Of course," Mary-Ellen agrees, not taking her eyes from me.

My cheeks are beginning to feel as though it's been dunked in hot sauce.

I push myself up from my seat, saying, "Well, it's been lovely seeing you both, but I—"

"And the way that strapping young man looks at you, dear? Mercy, mercy me," Mary-Ellen continues, her hand over her heart. "I was just telling Suzette here that when I saw him at the Drench for Defense, I swear I saw actual love hearts floating above his head when he looked at you, like a character on one of those cartoons Mabel used to watch."

"Mrs. McCluskey—" I begin, but I'm cut off.

"Not that we're judging you, mind. A woman needs companionship. Isn't that right, Suzette?"

"Especially a woman who's been through what you have with that awful Dwayne," Suzette agrees.

"Speaking of which, I'm sure I saw him at your place at the weekend. Is everything all right on that front, dear?" Mary-Ellen asks.

I need to put a stop to this, and I need to do it now.

"Look, I would love to answer all of your questions, ladies, but I really do have to go," I say, stepping away from the table.

"One more tiny question, Clara, for my own peace of mind," Mary-Ellen calls out.

For her peace of mind? More like for her gossip mill.

But I don't let her ask. Instead, I say a cheerful, "Bye now!"

and fly through the door, the rain instantly dampening my hair as I rush toward my car down the street.

As I close my car door over, I let out a breath. Why didn't I get Cade to park down the street where busybody neighbors wouldn't spot him so easily? Mary-Ellen just activated her personal broadcasting system, and I give it approximately six hours before this information reaches every household within a ten-mile radius.

Which gives further impetus to my task this morning.

I reach the office, my dampened hair beginning to curl, and the pumpkin cinnamon bun now too water damaged to offer Veronica. I dump it on my desk, say a quick hello to Millie, and without giving myself the chance to back down, I make my way to Veronica's office.

"Where's the fire?" Bailey says as I dash past her desk.

I come to a stop. "I'm going to tell Veronica now."

"About you know who?"

"I need to."

"Good luck. I'll be here if you need me," Bailey says.

"Thanks." I stride over to Veronica's office and clear my throat when I reach her open door.

She looks up at me from her computer screen. "Clara. How are you today? Feeling better?"

"I'm doing great, thanks. I got you a coffee." I place the cup on her desk, noticing a few drops of rainwater sliding from it and pooling around the rim. "Sorry. It's raining."

"Don't apologize. It's very thoughtful of you." She picks up the cup and takes a sip. "Falling for Books?"

"Maple Grounds."

"Ah."

"Can we talk?"

"Of course. Is it a door shut or door open kind of conversation?"

"Door shut." I turn and close the door over as a swoop of nerves zip through me. But I need to have this conversation, and after my experience just now with the gossipmongers of Maple Falls, it can't have come a moment too soon.

I sit on the other side of her desk and steel myself.

You've got this.

"Veronica, I need to tell you something," I begin, my pulse thudding, and instantly I wish I had taken up Cade's offer to be here with me. But I was determined to stand on my own two feet, full of self-righteous ownership of the situation, telling him it was my issue to deal with and not his. He doesn't have a non-fraternization clause in his contract. I do, and I need to step up—even if right now I wish he was here to lend his support.

"If it's about the latest metrics for the Hockey 101 series you've started, let me tell you, fans are loving your dynamic with Cade. He's all about fun and you're the one holding it together like a pro. You bounce off each other so nicely."

"It works, right?" I'd seen the success of the first video and knew she would be happy with the results. The comments were a mixture of hockey and the inevitable observations about Cade's and my chemistry. Now that I'm no longer working at ignoring my feelings for him, those comments simply make me smile. "That's not what I wanted to talk about, though."

"Oh?"

I take a deep breath and begin. "Let me preface it by saying how much I love this job and how grateful I am to you for giving me this opportunity."

She frowns. "You're not quitting, are you, Clara?"

"No. Nothing like that." *Although you might fire me when I tell you what I'm about to say.* "I came to see you because I need to tell you that although I didn't set out for this to happen, the fact of the matter is I've started a relationship with one of the players." I hold my breath, waiting for her reply.

She leans back in her chair, her fingers steepled, regarding me through narrowed eyes. "So, the rumors are true?"

My mind instantly darts to Mary-Ellen McCluskey.

"Rumors?"

"I overheard an older woman talking about you and Cade Lennox with her friends after the Drench for Defense on Saturday. A petite woman with short cropped grey hair and glasses. She was convinced you two were a thing. I dismissed it in my mind of course."

"That would be Mrs. McCluskey. She just questioned me at the bakery. She loves to gossip."

"But you're telling me in this case it's not gossip."

"It's not. I want to be transparent with you, Veronica. I don't want to hide anything from you."

She stares at me, her features unreadable. After a beat, she says, "Clara, you do know we have a non-fraternization policy at the Ice Breakers? Having any form of romantic relationship with someone employed here would be a breach of that policy."

"I do know that, and I want you to know that I never set out for this to happen. The truth of the matter is, Veronica, I fell in love."

Her eyes widen. "Love? You're in *love*?"

I nod my head slowly. "That's why I wanted to talk to you. This isn't just some fling. What Cade and I have is real."

"What Cade and you have goes against policy," she says pointedly, and my anxiety peaks.

"I know and I am so sorry for that. I love this job, and I would never willingly do anything to compromise it. I didn't go looking for love, but I found it anyway." I pull my laptop from my purse and open it onto the spreadsheet I prepared yesterday. "The team's social media engagement has improved significantly under my management. In fact, as you'll see here, there has been over a 400% increase in views on my most recent five videos alone, with comments and re-posting more than tripling. Veronica, I believe this shows that my relationship doesn't in any way compromise my ability to do my job, and to do it well. In fact, you were the one who encouraged me to work with Cade, and those videos have been especially popular with our fans."

She twists her mouth, her eyes still trained on me. "Your

performance to date has been commendable, and you're right, yours and Cade's campaigns have been particularly successful."

"I believe our dynamic on camera is a unique marketing asset to the Ice Breakers. Your encouragement to put myself in the frame proves my point."

"I did encourage you, it's true."

The "but" dangles in the air between us—and so do my chances.

She leans her elbows on her desk. "Clara, we have this policy for a reason."

Her words are like a pin prick to my balloon of hope.

"Do you remember the story I told you about Cade and the Blades team owner's daughter?"

I open my mouth to reply when there's a rap on the door, making me jump in surprise.

"I'm in a meeting," Veronica calls out, but whoever it is at the door isn't listening as it's nudged open, revealing the very topic of our conversation.

Cade.

He's in his practice gear, fresh from the ice, his hair damp with sweat, his bulk more than filling the doorway. As his soft eyes land on mine, my heart squeezes. *Hard.*

He's looking exactly like my fantasy of a knight in shining armor, except his armor is sweaty post-practice gear and that ever confident smile of his that suggests he's about to charm his way through my work crisis.

Part of me wants to sink through the floor in utter mortification.

Another part of me, the part that's been falling harder for this man every day, is beyond relieved that he disregarded my instruction to stay away. Facing Veronica's disappointment in me on my own was terrifying but facing it with Cade somehow makes it feel less something to fear and more something to simply try to navigate.

"I'm sorry to interrupt, Ms. Reynolds, but I could see you had

Clara in here with you, and I wanted to say something, if I may?" he asks.

Veronica sits up straighter in her chair, her eyes darting between us as her eyebrows climb toward her hairline. "Mr. Lennox, I wasn't aware this meeting was expanding to include additional participants."

Cade shrugs. "I figured you were talking about something close to my heart." His eyes dart to mine, his brows pulling together. "You were already talking about it, right, Triple?"

"We were," I say in a small voice, my heart formerly buoyed by the sight of him now taking a nosedive, knowing where the conversation was leading before he got here.

"Have a seat, Mr. Lennox," Veronica offers, and Cade lowers his bulk into the chair beside me. "Clara was telling me that things have developed beyond a professional relationship between you."

He slides his eyes to mine, flashing me a small smile. "That's right."

"Are you aware that this goes against Clara's contract? That there's a non-fraternization policy in there designed for these types of…situations?"

"She told me about that, and I wanted to tell you that this woman isn't just some fling to me, like Misty was all those years ago in New York." He turns to me, and my heart squeezes as I see nothing but sincerity in his eyes. "I'm in love with Clara Johnson, and I'll do whatever I need to protect that love."

He holds my gaze, and it's like Veronica, her office, the anxiety over my current job predicament slips away, and it's just him and me, together, a united front.

It feels freaking amazing.

"Well," Veronica says, pulling my attention from Cade. "This is certainly a more complex issue than I expected to face when I came to work this morning. Here's what's going to happen next. I need to discuss this with Paul and the executive team. This isn't a decision I can make unilaterally, no matter how compelling you both are." Her lips lift into a smile, and I know she can see that what we feel for one another is real.

"When will I know the outcome?" I ask.

"I'd say Monday morning. In the meantime, nothing changes. Tomorrow's Inaugural Bash proceeds as planned, and I expect you to capture footage as usual."

I nod, my insides twisting like they're trying to tie themselves in knots. "I guess that's it then?"

"That's it," she confirms.

Cade and I both rise to our feet, and he places his hand lightly against my lower back to lead me from the room.

"Clara? Cade?"

We look back at Veronica.

"For what it's worth, I'm happy for you both. It's hard to find love in this cynical world, and by the looks of you, you've found it in one another."

Cade reaches for my hand, and we share a smile.

Monday morning feels like both a lifetime away and terrifyingly imminent, but as Cade's thumb traces across my knuckles, I realize something important has shifted in my life. For the first time in many, many years, I'm not facing an uncertain future alone. Whatever the executive team decides, whatever consequences await me, we will handle them together.

CHAPTER 18
CADE

WE PARK outside the sports facility's ballroom for the Ice Breakers' Inaugural Bash in our black tie best, me in a black tux with a crisp white shirt, and Clara in a deep blue, flowy dress that's both sexy as heck and somehow kind of regal. It hugs her just right at the waist and dips low enough to make me forget what I was saying when she pulled the door open at her house. It's simple, classy, and totally distracting.

She steps out of my car and smooths the skirt of her dress with her palms, looking up at me with an uncertain look in her eyes.

"We've got this, Triple," I tell her as I pull her against me, planting a kiss on her forehead. "And did I mention how incredible you look tonight?"

Her pillowy lips lift into a smile. "Only about seven times."

"Let's make it eight. You look breathtakingly beautiful tonight, my love."

She looks at me like I just handed her the stars. "I love it when you call me that."

"My love? I only call you that because I'm in love with you."

She laughs. "That's a good enough reason, and you look beyond handsome in your tux."

"Gotta look good for my woman," I say in a caveman voice, which makes her laugh some more. I look over at the banner that reads *Ice Breakers Inaugural Bash – Welcome to Maple Falls* in letters so big you could read them from a plane at 30,000 feet. "I suppose we'd better get in there."

"I suppose we had." Her expression drops, and I know what she's feeling. Trepidation. Fear. She could lose her job come Monday, which is so much more than just a job to her. It represents her independence and strength, her journey to reclaim her strength from her CFS and from her manipulative catfish of an ex.

Not that I want to go thinking about Dwayne Campbell on a night like this. Just the mere thought of him makes my blood boil, and if Clara would let me, I would tell him exactly what I think of the guy. He's scum. End of story.

But she told me that she won't let me fight all her battles, and I get that.

I'd still love to give that jerk a piece of my mind.

"Come on. We've got this," I say, and together we make our way across the parking lot. They've rolled out an actual red carpet at the entrance, which is flanked by hay bales and fancy fall flowers, giving it a small-town flair. We pose for a few photos before we head inside.

Clara shrugs off her coat, and I pass it to the coat check and take the chance to drink her in once more. Clara is always beautiful to me, whether she's in her sweats, lying low at home on her sofa, her hair in a messy bun, or in her slim-fitted skirts and modest blouses for work. But tonight? Tonight, she's next level beautiful, and my heart is bursting with love for her as she slides her arm through mine, throwing me one final nervous look before we merge into the crowd.

The ballroom has been transformed into what looks like what happens when you give a decorator an unlimited budget and a serious obsession with ice. Ice Breakers team colors are on every surface, and whoever was in charge of this event clearly subscribed to the "go big or go home" school of event planning.

But you know what? It looks great, and it makes me feel proud to be a part of this team, this community, and this town I now call home.

The place is packed. I'm told Maple Falls has ten thousand residents, and I'm betting at least nine thousand of them are crammed in here tonight.

"There's Keira and Bailey," Clara says. "Let's go say hi."

We make our way through the crowd, and I shake hands with Lucian, Weston, and Carson, all dressed up like me in their penguin suits, before we reach Clara's sister and her friend, Bailey. Like Clara, Keira is in a floor-length dress, hers green, her hair in loose curls.

"Oh, my gosh, Clara. You look so gorgeous!" Keira exclaims as she and Clara hug.

"*I* look gorgeous? Look at you! I love what you did with your hair," Clara replies. "And Bailey, look at you! So beautiful." She pulls her friend into a hug.

"Right back atcha," Bailey replies.

"You all look crazy hot," I say.

"Thanks, Cade," Bailey says with a grin, and I take Clara's hand in mine, giving it a reassuring squeeze.

With her job hanging in the balance, I need to be there for her every step of the way, which includes giving her encouraging touches. Which, let's be real, isn't exactly a hardship for a man newly in love.

Bailey and Keira both flick their gaze to our joined hands.

"Do you need to tell us something?" Keira asks.

"You guys are going public now?" Bailey adds.

"We told my boss yesterday morning," Clara explains.

"Wow. That's a big move," Keira replies. "How did it go?"

"Well, it was meant to be just me, but someone decided to crash the party." She shoots me a mock serious look, and I shrug, happy with my decision to turn up to Clara and Veronica's meeting yesterday. I wanted to be there for her, and for a straightforward guy like me, that means *literally*.

"And?" her sister leads.

"And Veronica has taken it to Paul Vaughn, the CEO. My new career as the social media manager for the Ice Breakers is hanging in the balance tonight."

Keira's jaw slackens. "So, you don't know if you still have a job?" Clara gives a small shake of her head, and Keira rubs her arm. "Oh, babe. I'm so sorry. You're in total limbo right now. That's terrible."

Terrible is right. But I have a plan, and I'm going to put it into action tonight.

Afterall, Clara's happiness matters so much to me, and after what she's been through with "he who shall not be named"—yup, I just Voldemort-ed Dwayne Campbell, although seriously, the guy makes Voldemort look like Prince Charming—Clara needs whatever I can give her.

And I want to give Clara the world.

"Sometimes you've got to hold tight to the things that matter, and deal with the consequences," Bailey says, and Clara nods.

"That's what we're doing," I reply, smiling down at this beautiful woman I get to call mine. She smiles back up at me, and it makes my heart squeeze in my chest.

"Where's Dan?" Clara asks her sister, but she doesn't have the chance to respond as Troy Hart, the arena and team owner, steps up to the mic, Coach Hauser flanking him like a body-guard, and the crowd falls into silence.

"Catch you soon." Clara gives my hand a squeeze before she slips away, pulling her phone from her purse, ready to record. Troy begins his speech by assuring everyone that we're headed for an incredible season, puffing out his chest like he's personally suiting up for game one.

I get his passion. Troy Hart once played in the League, and he wants our new team to be a success, as does the rest of the town. I also happen to agree with him. We may be new, we may have been a disparate group of players not that long ago, more used to battling it out against one another on the ice than working together to win, but we have some serious talent on the team, and a drive to achieve big things.

Coach Hauser says a few rousing words, taken right from the coach's inspirational handbook, and when they wrap up, the room erupts like we just won the Cup, the cheers, hoots, and applause practically shaking the walls.

"Everyone believes in this new team," Keira says as a waiter offers a tray of drinks.

I pick up a glass of water and take a sip.

"No champagne to celebrate?" Keira asks, lifting a flute to her lips.

"Can't. The first game's in four days, and Coach is pretty clear about us not drinking during the season, just like my Blades coach."

"So, you and Clara are together now," Keira says.

It's not a question.

"She deserves a good guy, and you're a good guy, right, Cade?" She gives me a questioning look, and I know she's being protective of her sister. I may not be the guy I once was, but the rest of the world doesn't know that.

Not yet anyway.

"I know I haven't known Clara all that long, and people might be suspicious of a guy like me, with the reputation I've got. But you can trust me when I say, I'm in love with your sister, and I will do anything to protect that love. You have my word."

"But what about all those stories about you being a womanizer? You're not exactly known as a steady relationship kinda guy, by the looks of things, and Clara has Benny and Hannah. She's a package deal."

"I gave up that lifestyle a long time ago, only the world hasn't quite cottoned on." I lean in a little closer to her. "Keira, I know you're Clara's sister and you love her, but please believe me when I say I'm all in with her. *All* in."

She studies me for a beat, and I'm hoping she hears the sincerity in my words. When she finally opens her mouth to speak, her features have softened. "I believe you," she says softly, her lips tilting upward. "Just make sure you treat her right. Got it?"

I grin at her because I have every intention of treating Clara right. "I promise."

"Good," she replies simply before taking a sip of her drink.

Asher catches my eye and makes his way past a few people to us. We shake hands, slapping each other on the back, before I introduce him to Keira.

"I know you. You're the one who threw the bucket of water over this guy at the Drench for Defense," Asher says.

Keira lifts her hands up in the air, grinning. "Guilty."

"Nice shot, by the way," Asher says. "So, you're Dan Roberts's wife, right?"

"And Clara's sister," Keira replies, throwing me a meaningful look.

"Clara's sister, huh?" Asher says, also shooting me a look. "Cade knows Clara pretty well, from what I hear. Right, Cade?" he teases.

I slap him on the shoulder once more. "You might be my teammate, but off the ice you're just a guy who uses my gym."

He chortles and I glance at the stage where Troy Hart and Coach Hauser just gave their speeches. "As much as I'd like to stay here and get grilled by you, I've got something pressing I need to do."

"You know I know where you live, right?" Asher says with a sardonic grin.

I shake my head at him. "You've used my gym more than once. Remember, old man?"

He barks out a laugh at my jest. But he doesn't know the full story. Not yet, anyway. He doesn't know I turned over the leaf I knew I needed to do by moving to this town.

And turning that leaf led me to the love I now have.

"Catch you both later," I say as I make my way through the crowd.

Stepping up onto the stage, I scan the crowd for Clara. She isn't hard to spot, her blonde hair catching the light, glowing like gold. She's speaking with Veronica and the guy I recognize as Paul Vaughn, CEO of the Ice Breakers.

The tautness of her features tells me everything I need to know.

I stride over to the microphone and tap it a few times, making a banging sound that reverberates around the room, bouncing off the walls.

A few heads turn to look my way, and I clear my throat. "Hey, everyone," I say into the mic, feeling like I'm about to jump off a cliff without checking for a safe landing below. A hush falls gradually over the crowd. "For those of you who don't know me, my name is Cade Lennox and I'm a winger for this awesome new NHL team we're celebrating here tonight."

I pause, watching Clara go pale as she watches me, wondering what I'm doing.

Sorry, Triple, but sometimes you've got to go all-in when the stakes are high.

Because this is about me and Clara, and the man I've become.

"I'm not that good at this sort of thing, but I've got something to say, and I hope you'll give me the chance to say it."

There's a murmur that rumbles around the room before it falls to silence.

I clear my throat. "I bet I can guess what most of you think about me. Pro hockey player, am I right? Big contract, bigger ego, probably goes through women like I go through hockey sticks."

There are a few chuckles that ripple through the crowd, and I can practically feel my teammates cringing somewhere out there.

"And to be honest, for a long time, that guy you're thinking of *was* me."

The room has gone completely silent now, all eyes on me, which is either really good or totally catastrophic.

Me? I don't take my eyes from Clara's, her features creased in worry as she hangs on my every word.

"But here's the thing. I'm not that guy anymore. Haven't been for some time, in fact. Moving here to this town, joining this team? It was to give myself the space to explore the man I knew I could be."

Mary-Ellen McCluskey is practically vibrating with excitement in the front row, and I'm sure this moment is going to fuel Maple Falls gossip for the next year.

"The truth is, I've fallen in love with the most wonderful woman, and it's the kind of love that means I'm willing to make a total fool of myself in front of the whole town."

"You're proving that part all right!" some guy calls out, but I won't let him break my stride. I've got something to say, and I'm going to say it.

"The woman I love is smart, and funny, and strong. Strong enough to rebuild her entire life from scratch. Someone I'm proud to say loves me back." I take a breath. "That someone is Clara Johnson."

Gasps burst from the crowd, and people swivel their heads in Clara's direction. She's watching me, her eyes intense.

"I knew it!" Mary-Ellen McCluskey calls out.

I pull my lips into a line. "The problem is, because of me, Clara's job is now at risk."

There are more murmurs, but this time, I push on.

"So, here's my proposal to team management. If Clara loses her job because I was stupid enough to fall in love with her, the most amazing woman I've ever met, I'm stepping down from my contract. I'll pay the penalties. I don't care. For the first time in my life, I've found something more important than hockey, and I'm not going to let it go."

The silence is deafening, and all I can hear is my own heartbeat, thrashing in my ears.

But I've said what I needed to say, and now the cards will fall where they fall.

A blur of blue and gold pushes through the crowd. "Excuse me. Excuse me. Excuse me," a voice says, and it takes me a moment to realize it's Clara, urgently making her way to me.

She steps up onto the stage and gives an embarrassed wave at the guests before hurrying across to me. She places her hand over the microphone and immediately a loud piercing shriek sounds around the room.

She snaps her hand away. "Sorry, everyone. I didn't mean to do that. I just wanted a quiet word with Cade."

"I think we would all like to hear what you have to say to that romantic declaration," Mrs. McCluskey calls out and there's a murmur of agreement among the crowd.

"Really? Because it's kinda just between him and me," Clara replies.

"Come on, Clara. Say your piece," Mrs. McCluskey instructs.

She shoots me a brief look before she lowers the microphone to her height, and says, "I just wanted to say that what Cade said is amazing, and I love him all the more for it." She smiles at me and my heart sings. "But the thing is, I get to keep my job."

"You do?" I ask, dumbfounded.

She nods, her big blue eyes pooling with tears. Happy tears. Tears of joy. "Paul just told me."

I reach for her hand. "I love you," I say, and she says it right back, her eyes like fire as she gazes at me.

"What about the no fraternities policy?" Mrs. McCluskey asks.

"It's not about fraternities, Mary-Ellen," her friend corrects, another older lady, dressed to the nines in a black velvet dress and a huge, sparkling necklace. "It's a non-flirtation policy. Isn't that right, Clara?"

Clara bites back a laugh. "It's called a non-fraternization clause, and my bosses, Veronica Reynolds, and Paul Vaughn, have agreed that they can make an exception for me." She squeezes my hand, smiling up at me. "For us."

"Seriously?" I ask, and I feel as giddy as a tween meeting his hockey idol.

"Seriously," she confirms.

And then I do the most natural thing in the world. I reach out and collect the woman I love in my arms, pressing a blistering kiss against her soft lips. I get lost in her, the woman I'm lucky enough to call mine, until the sound of whoops and whistles puncture our little bubble, and together, we turn to look out at the crowd.

"Show's over," I tell them with a grin. I wrap my arm around Clara's shoulders and together we climb down from the stage, and out the exit, into the empty corridor.

"So, you keep your job? You're sure?" I ask again, just to be safe.

"I do."

"And I don't have to quit?"

"Of course you don't. Honey, I had no idea you were going to do that."

I grin at her as I scoop her up in my arms once more, feeling her soft curves melding against me, right where they belong. "You're worth it," I murmur against her lips before I claim them once more, wrapped up in the most emotional kiss of my life, right here in the town I call home, with the woman I love.

CHAPTER 19
CLARA

THE ATMOSPHERE in the arena is electric as I lead Benny and Hannah, with hotdogs in hand, to find our seats for the very first game of the season. All three of us are wearing a very special name and number on our hockey jerseys, a gift from the man himself, and I could not be prouder.

I spot familiar face after familiar face as we make our way through the crowd, saying hello to friends and neighbors. By now, I know it would take a small miracle for them not to know about Cade and me. With Mary-Ellen McCluskey and Suzette Donnelly directing traffic on the Maple Falls gossip superhighway, there's next to no hope they don't.

"Hello, Clara. Hi, kids," my friend and fellow Chronic Warriors battler, Marianne says as she gives me a quick hug. "You're all looking so good in your matching jerseys."

"It's Cade's jersey. He gave them to us all," Hannah replies.

"We're team Lennox," I say with a shrug.

Marianne's eyes brighten. "I heard about that. Good for you."

"Mrs. McCluskey?" I ask.

Her eyes dance. "How did you know?"

"Call it a wild guess."

"Here you go, honey," a man says as he passes Marianne a bowl of fries, and I do a double take when I recognize him.

"Martin?" I question, my gaze bouncing between the two bickering support group members.

"Hey, Clara. What are you doing here?" he replies, his shoulders hunching, as if trying to duck under my scrutiny.

"They've come to watch the game, of course," Marianne replies as her cheeks color.

"So, you two...?" I flick my index finger between them, and Marianne lifts her chin.

"You young people with your hockey players don't have a monopoly on love, you know," she replies, her lips quirking as she turns her gaze on Martin.

He slips a hand into hers and smiles back at her.

"I always wondered about you two. I'm very happy for you both," I say.

"Mommy, let's go!" Benny says, tugging on my sleeve.

"Enjoy the game. Go Ice Breakers!" I say as we move away.

"Go Ice Breakers!" they call back.

We find our row right by the plexiglass, just one of the perks of dating a player. I greet Keira and Dan as we shimmy past them.

"Looking good, you guys," Keira says as I settle in beside her.

"I thought we wore my number as a family," Dan says with a mock serious look.

"That was before she fell in love with the team's new star winger," Keira explains to her husband.

All I do is smile at them, blissful in the knowledge that I'm wearing the right man's number, the *only* man's number.

44.

Officially, it's a new number for him, representing his fresh start, both on this team and in life.

Privately, he shared with me that he chose 44 because it's a pair of two equal numbers, representing him and me.

It'll come as no surprise that I dissolved into tears with that particular gesture.

But right now, the feeling is less "emotional sobbing because my boyfriend did something incredibly romantic for me," and more "Go Ice Breakers!!" for their first game of the season, right here at the arena in Maple Falls.

We have an official videographer capturing all the footage for our socials, so I've got the evening off to be with my family, supporting the team I both love and work for—and the man I still can't believe is mine.

"What's Cade saying the team's chances are tonight?" Dan asks me, raising his voice over the excited crowd. "The Great Lake Vikings are a solid team."

"Word says it'll be a tough start to the season for the guys, but the Ice Breakers might just have the advantage," I reply.

"Is that wishful thinking because your new boyfriend is on the team?" Keira teases with a nudge and a smirk.

"No, it's faith in the team," I insist before I cave, oh so quickly. "And because my new boyfriend's on the team."

She grins at me. "I knew it."

A gray head turns to look up at me, and I recognize Mary-Ellen McCluskey. She's sitting with her husband, Murray, both of them in Ice Breaker colors. "Oh, hello there, Clara, kids. Your sister told me you were coming tonight, and I'm so happy to see you."

"It's lovely to see you, too, Mrs. McCluskey," I reply.

"I'm so glad you're here. I've been dying to tell you what I heard about your dreadful ex-husband yesterday," she begins, and I know she's about to launch into her story, whether I want to hear it or not. She rises to her feet and indicates for me to lean closer to her, presumably so the kids don't hear. Dwayne may be a catfishing jerk with questionable morals, but he's still their dad. I want to protect them from anything that could damage their relationship with him.

I get the feeling he's managing that quite well on his own.

"My friend, Doreen, lives in Portland and she heard from her sister, Carlene—isn't that funny the way their names almost rhyme? What were their parents thinking?" She glances at the kids, who are too preoccupied with taking in the packed arena and munching on their hotdogs to pay her any attention.

"Anyway, Carlene lives in the same building as your ex and Izzy Barlowe, that despicable former friend of yours who ran off with your husband," she clarifies, as though I might not remember who Izzy Barlowe is. "She told Doreen that Izzy found out about him trying to woo some woman online, and do you know what she did?" she asks, but she doesn't wait for my response, the question clearly rhetorical, the gossip too juicy not to spill. "She threw him out! Right onto the street! Carlene said she put all his things in trash bags, too. You know the sort, those big ones you can fit a lot into? She threw them out, too, right from their third-floor condo." She pauses long enough to take a breath, her features alight with glee. "One of the bags split open on impact, sending his shoes and other items of clothing flying."

"She threw him out?" I ask, aghast. Aghast and a touch elated, if I'm honest.

Okay, *a lot* elated.

Dwayne had gotten away with not only treating me and the kids horribly, but Izzy, too, thanks to his little dalliance with me as ChronicWarrior88. If what Mrs. McCluskey is saying is true, he's finally getting a little dose of what he deserves.

Mrs. McCluskey nods, her lips terse. "Dreadful man! You're

well rid of him, Clara. Well rid! And you know what? Poor Carlene found a pair of your ex's boxer shorts on her windshield the very next day, can you believe? Poor woman thought she had some kind of sick stalker who liked to leave his personal clothing for women to find before she worked out they were Dwayne's."

"Wow."

Mrs. McCluskey may be the town gossip, but she's nearly always correct in her knowledge, even if sometimes details are, shall we say, "expanded" for dramatic means. She's a fully paid subscriber of the "don't ever let the truth get in the way of a good story" club, that's for sure.

"So, Clara, what do you think of that?" She leans back on her feet, a satisfied look on her face.

I shake my head, the story soaking in. "I don't know quite what to think, Mrs. McCluskey." A thought occurs to me. "Is Dwayne okay?"

She throws her hands on her hips. "Clara Johnson. I tell you a story that should have you feeling avenged in at least a small way, and all you ask is whether that rat of an ex of yours is okay?"

I flick my gaze to Benny and Hannah, who still seem totally oblivious of our conversation, still enjoying their hotdogs and watching the crowd. "I'm only asking for the kids' sake."

She smiles, her features softening. "Of course you are. And the answer to your question is I don't know, and nor do I think you should care."

"That's quite a story."

Her eyes light up. "Isn't it? I do love it when a bad guy gets his comeuppance. Enjoy the game, watching your new beau."

"I will." She takes her seat once more and I sit back in mine. I'm fairly sure I'm the woman Izzy caught Dwayne chatting with online, but it could have been someone else. He could have been trying to seduce a whole raft of women, for all I know.

What I do know is I no longer care. Dwayne will always be

the kids' dad, and so he'll be in my life in some form or another for many years to come.

But I'm not the person I once was when I fell in love with him.

I'm not the person I was when he left me.

I'm strong. I'm confident. I'm capable of so much.

And I've got a man who cherishes and supports every aspect of me: the good, the bad, and the chronically fatigued.

"What did Mrs. McCluskey have to say?" Keira asks, and I tell her the story of Dwayne and his belongings being summarily dumped by Izzy.

"It couldn't have happened to a nicer guy," she says with a satisfied grin.

"These guys are making history tonight," Dan says, his eyes shining.

"They sure are, honey, just like you did when you captained the charity team," Keira says.

An announcer calls over the loudspeaker, "Ladies and gentlemen, welcome to the inaugural home game of your NHL Maple Falls Ice Breakers!"

The stadium roars, people rising to **their feet,** waving the merchandise and stomping **their feet**, really getting into the excitement of the event. The kids and I stand, along with Dan and Keira, every local grinning from ear to ear, proud that Maple Falls has its own NHL team, even if the future of the town is still hanging in the balance.

But all of that feels like a problem for another day as the town comes together to support our team, a town brought together by adversity, hoping for a victory on the ice tonight.

The announcer introduces the Great Lakes Vikings, and as the team members slide onto the ice one by one, most people applaud, their supporters showing their love for the team, but some people boo and call out, as well.

I feel a tug on my sleeve and look down to see Benny frowning up at me. "Why are they booing, Mommy?"

"Because they're the Great Lake Vikings, sweetheart. That's the team we want to beat today."

"Boo!" he calls out, and I resist telling him it's not exactly good sportsmanship to boo the opposition, but I don't. Not only is half the crowd doing it, but he's lapping up every minute of this game, and I don't want to do anything to dim his light.

"And now, the moment you've all been waiting for. Introducing your Maple Falls Ice Breakers!" the announcer declares, and immediately, the team's theme song, "Ice Ice Baby," begins to blare and people start to dance.

As each skater is announced, I watch for Cade. I don't need to wait long.

"And on the right wing is Cade Lennox!" the announcer says, and we cheer and wave, and after skating out and waving at the crowd, he turns to where he knows we're sitting and throws us a wave, his massive grin reaching from ear to ear.

I wave back as my heart swells with love for this beautiful man who came into my life and changed it for the better. He winks at me before he skates across the ice to join his team, as though he's as light as a feather.

"Who knew we'd both end up with hockey players?" Keira says, and my heart squeezes at the thought I could end up with Cade. Not just his girlfriend, but maybe, someday, his wife.

Just as quickly as the thought occurs to me, I know what my answer would be.

Yes.

Not that I want to rush what we have. We fell in love fast, and even though my heart knows he's everything I want, everything I need, I'm happy with where we are right now. We are two people newly in love, spending whatever free time we can together, learning more and more about each other every day.

And it's the best feeling in the world.

The whole team is now on the ice, and soon enough, play begins, and we take our seats, waiting for the story of the Ice Breakers' first ever NHL game to unfold.

The two teams move around the ice with blistering speed, smashing into one another with the kind of mayhem that makes the game of hockey both terrifying and addictive to watch.

A mere handful of minutes after the starting sound, Asher Tremblay, my new Chronic Warriors buddy, gets the first goal of the game. I leap to my feet, cheering him on with the rest of the supporters as the goal horn blares and the team song sounds out around the arena. The crowd goes nuclear with excitement.

There's another goal to the Ice Breakers in the first period, thanks to Carson Crane's handiwork, and the tension in the arena is evident among not only the Ice Breakers fans, but the fans of the Vikings, too. Our team is up 2-0, and I for one am quietly confident we can dig deep and keep the opposition from scoring. I know how much this new team wants a victory.

We take our seats, both the tension and expectation high. The play is as fast and as brutal as it was in the first, and my heart is in my mouth as I watch, riveted to the action on the ice with an intensity I've not experienced before.

But then I've never before been in love with one of the players out there battling it out.

No goals come in the second, though not from the want of trying as both teams vie for the period dominance. Thankfully, the Ice Breakers keep the opposition shutout.

As we wait for the third period, Dan leans over and says, "I bet Coach Hauser will be telling the guys to keep it tight in the third. He won't want any heroics or exhibition hockey unless they have a clear and concise shot on goal."

"Let's hope they don't get that chance," I reply, my nerves pinging.

Then the teams come back onto the ice for the final period to rapturous applause. The energy buzzing around the whole arena is electric, and we can almost taste the victory within our grasp.

Our home fans are showing their allegiance to their new team.

Play begins and Cade gets the puck. Instantly, I grip the edge of my seat, my heart hammering against my ribs with each bone-jarring check along the boards.

Even from my spot behind the plexiglass, I can see his look of dogged determination, the expression of a man with single minded resolve to make his mark on this game.

He begins to weave through defenders like the players are in a dance choreographed just for him. Beside me, Benny says, "Look, Mommy! Cade's got the puck and he's close to the goal!"

My heart is beating with adrenaline as the frenetic pace of the game seems to slow, and it's like every person in the arena is holding a collective breath as Cade lines up the shot, his wind-up as smooth as silk, precise and perfectly timed.

And then *boom*! His stick makes bruising contact with the puck, launching it like a cannon, slicing through the air. The goalie dives to block it, misses, the puck sailing past him, the force of Cade's slapshot sending it right into the back of the net.

For a split second, the entire arena falls to silence before the goal horn sounds and the Ice Breaker fans jump up, screaming and cheering, and stomping their feet in jubilation, me and Hannah and Benny and Keira and Dan along with them. All of us are united in the captivating force of this team, sailing to a 3-0 lead over the Vikings.

There's something so primal, so raw about watching someone you love overcome the opposition and succeed spectacularly in a bruising athletic pursuit in front of thousands of people. And you know what? It's a feeling I could get used to, and if Cade plays like he has tonight, I may well need to.

I don't take my eyes from him, watching as he raises his stick in the air in celebration, gliding across the ice, a broad grin plastered across his face. His teammates pile on top of him, congratulating him on his incredible shot. He emerges from the huddle, gliding over to our side of the ice, when he raises his stick and taps the plexiglass, his gaze capturing mine as he mouths, "For you."

My heart leaps, and as Keira nudges me with her elbow, I

gaze back at Cade with the goofiest grin, and I swear something just did a joyful leap somewhere south of my ribs.

I'm in love with a man who can make an entire building lose its collective mind with a single shot, a man who I once wrote off as an overgrown man-child. A tear slips down my cheek as the arena continues to roar around us, the celebration feeling like it might go on forever.

Watching the man I love triumph, not just on the ice, but in claiming us in as public a way as his victory feels like the culmination of everything we've fought for. I press my hand to my heart, feeling it thunder beneath my palm. I know that no matter what challenges await us, no matter what the future holds, we've already won something far more precious than any game.

We've won each other.

CHAPTER 20
CADE

CRAMMING this many people into Clara's home was going to be like trying to fit the entire Ice Breakers team onto a Zamboni, which is why we're all here at my place today. The November sun is weak in the sky, the large windows showcasing the view of the trees, bathed in soft light. The football game on the big screen above the fireplace is on, even though no one's paying much attention to it, my living room full of family, both Clara's and mine, congregated here today to celebrate Thanksgiving.

Looking around at the quiet chaos, I've come a long way since last Thanksgiving, when I was totally over the life I'd created for myself, contemplating a move to this small town in Washington state I now call home. Now, I cannot imagine having a Thanksgiving any other way.

Benny is showing my nephew, Oliver, his Max Griffin toy— once a "collectible" but since having spent the last two months out of its packaging, going on adventures with Benny including ending up in the bathtub a couple times, definitely reduced to "toy" status—telling him all about *The Timekeeper Chronicles* and why Max is the hero of the series. Oliver is a few years younger than Benny and is hanging on his every word. I make myself a mental note to talk to Oliver later. Everyone knows the true hero of the comic book series isn't a hero at all but a heroine by the name of Zara Kazan.

I think Benny and I will have to choose to disagree on that one.

Hannah is in her full-on big sister mode, sitting at Bess as she shows my niece, Olivia, how to play the Taylor Swift song "Enchanted" that she and I played together for Show Quest a few days ago. Helping her overcome her stage fright was such a satisfying feeling for me, and yeah, it was pretty dang good when Clara's dropkick of an ex got all antsy with me after the show about it. Well, not to my face exactly. I find guys like him with the big talk and swagger rarely front up in person.

Coward.

Hannah didn't win the overall event. That honor went to Leo Garibaldi, although I've already agreed with Hannah, we'll do our darndest to beat him next year. But she did win Best Duet, and she insisted I get up on the stage with her to receive her award.

I'm not going to lie. It felt amazing.

My sister Tori, her husband Lionel, and my mom are still a little starstruck despite having been here for the last hour, although it's not just thanks to me, Dawson Hayes, or Dan Roberts, the resident hockey pros in the room. Dan and Emmy's brother, Ethan, is here and not only is he a huge Netflix star on one of my favorite shows, *It Came One Winter*, but his wife is a princess. As in a literal princess. King and queen for parents, a sister-in-law who's a queen of a country called Malveaux, and a tiara collection the women have shown way too much interest in.

That said, Princess Amelia is a total sweetheart and is as down to earth as the rest of us, even if her life is a little more *gold-plated state dinner* than *pizza night in sweatpants*.

Clara is adding a layer of marshmallows to the deep dish filled with yams, and I come up behind her, sliding my hands around her little waist and breathing in her soft floral scent. "Mind if I take one?" I ask, reaching onto the marshmallow bag.

But she's too quick for me, pulling the bag away before I can dip into it, spinning around in my arms.

"How many times do I have to tell you? You'll spoil your appetite," she teases, her eyes sparkling with mirth.

I throw her my best smile, which she's been known to describe as "knee-weakening," much to my delight. "Please may I have one?" I say, adjusting my hold on her so I can feel her soft curves pressed against me.

"Since you asked so nicely." She reaches up and places a marshmallow in my mouth, and I bite down on it, enjoying its soft, gooey sweetness, my eyes trained on her. "You tried one of these?"

"I don't want to spoil *my* appetite," she replies.

"You should, Triple. They're delicious. I've got an idea." I lean down and press a sweet, marshmallow-y kiss against her soft lips.

"Mm. You're right, honey. Delicious," she murmurs.

It's been the best part of two months since I inadvertently made a fool of myself at the Inaugural Bash when I made my big announcement that I would walk away from my contract with the Ice Breakers if Clara lost her job over our relationship. I got ribbed mercilessly by the guys for weeks after, but you know what? I would do it all again because I meant every word of it. I would have walked away if Management had been short sighted enough to let Clara go. That's how much she means to me.

Since then, our love has only deepened, and spending time with not only the woman I love, but with her kids, too, has shown me what I missed out on all those years. I was so busy dodging commitment and not allowing myself to feel anything for a woman beyond attraction, now that I have it, I feel sorry for that guy. That kind of lifestyle can only last so long before it begins to feel empty, and now, looking out at our blended family, I know I'm exactly where I want to be.

"Hey, you two. This is a family show," Dawson says as he steals a marshmallow from the bag and quickly returns to the living room.

"I can't help it," I reply with a shrug. "Clara's the woman of my dreams." She snort laughs. "What?"

"You're telling me the woman of your dreams has next to no money, two kids, a horrible ex, and CFS?"

"Now that you mention it…"

She bats me playfully on the arm and I plant another kiss on her totally kissable lips. "I told you, Triple, you're everything I've ever wanted."

"That's better."

A short while later, with the candied yams in the oven, the turkey is almost finished cooking, and the rest of the meal ready to go, we join the rest of the family in the living room.

"So, tell me, Ami, do you have servants and live in an actual palace in Ledonia?" Tori asks Princess Amelia, who turned up in jeans and an Ice Breakers hoodie and insisted we all call her Ami the moment she stepped through the door.

"We do, although they're more like family, really, Theresa, my lady's maid, in particular," she replies.

"You have a lady's maid?" Tori's eyes are the size of pucks. "You're so *Downton Abbey*."

"They weren't royal, honey," Mom corrects.

"Or *real*," Ami says with a laugh. "Theresa and I have the

best gossip fests. She's always telling me what goes on in the servants' quarters. I tell you, we royals are dull by comparison. So much gossip."

"Didn't your brother give up his crown to marry a Texan princess?" Mom asks.

"Didn't your sister fall in love with the brother of the guy she was meant to marry?" Emmy asks.

"Don't forget the fact we met when you had run away from the palace," Ethan adds.

"I didn't say we were dull, did I?" Ami replies with a smile, her eyes dancing, and from what I know about her family, they sure aren't dull.

"That's for sure," Tori replies with a laugh.

"I heard a rumor," Keira says. "Cade got Asher to bid on him at the Bachelor Auction, using Cade's money—and won a date with himself! Is that right, Cade?"

"Sure is," I say without missing a beat.

"Why? Did you worry no one else would bid?" Ethan asks with a laugh.

Dan shakes his head. "Tragic, Lennox. Tragic."

"What can I say? I'm not as popular as I once was, and I like it that way," I reply as I flash a smile at Clara.

Knowing that Clara didn't have the funds to bid on me for the forty-five minute date to raise money to save Maple Falls, I got Asher to bid, using my money. She and I had already been together for a while when the Bachelor Auction came around, and I didn't want to go on a date with anyone else, even if it was for charity. And besides, I was happy to donate the money to the worthy cause of saving this town I now call home. This town I want to stay in past the end of this season and beyond.

Yup, I've made the call. I'm sticking around with the Ice Breakers for as long as they'll have me, making Maple Falls my permanent home. I've told Mom I'll move her across the country if she wants to live in Maple Falls, on one proviso: she stays well away from Mary-Ellen McCluskey and her gossip super-highway.

Mom's dangled a rather big carrot: she'll move to Maple Falls when Clara and I have kids.

When I told Clara, I wasn't sure what to expect. Would she widen her eyes in shock, telling me there was no way she was ever having any more kids? Or would she fall into my arms, telling me she couldn't imagine *not* having kids with me?

I was ecstatic to find out it was the latter, and although I'm not diving into marriage with her just yet, I have commissioned a ring I know will be perfect for Clara when the time is right.

And I have the feeling that time will be soon.

Although I don't know if they'll sell, I'm planning to approach the O'Connors to make this place my home. Our home, eventually. I'm hoping they'll say yes. You see, with six bedrooms, there's plenty of room for Clara, her kids, and any more kids who might come along in the future.

Yeah, I've become *that* guy, the one who's got his life all mapped out. But you know what? I could not be happier being that guy, looking at a wonderful future full of love ahead.

"You must be pleased with the Ice Breakers stats so far this season," Dan says, and I'm happy to move the conversation on.

"Yeah, I am," I reply. "We've won most of our games so far, with one draw and a loss. That one hurt."

"Pretty good for the newest team in the League, I'd say," Dawson says.

"Not to boast, but the Ice Hawks have a perfect record so far this season," Dan says, looking proud.

"Which city are they from?" Mom asks, and a few of us laugh. "What? I haven't heard of them before."

"It's my high school team," Dan explains. "I'm coaching them, and I tell you, there's some serious talent on that team, hence the perfect season so far. I'm seeing big things for this team."

"Don't get ahead of yourself yet, honey. There's still plenty of games to come," Keira says.

"And the best news? The town has been saved, too," Clara adds. "I got a message from Ashlyn earlier today."

"That's amazing news!" Dan says.

"You should definitely have led with that," I add.

"It seems like we've got a lot to be thankful for this year," Mom says, and I smile at her when she captures my gaze. I know how much it means for Mom to see me settled and happy. Although she didn't voice her concerns at the time, she said she was always worried about me and my lifestyle, secretly hoping I would meet a woman who would make such an impression on me I would change my ways. But it was me who changed before I met the woman, and that's why I was ready for her. Ready and open to love.

A short while later, with the food piping hot on the table, we all sit, with Clara and me serving up as everyone continues to chatter amongst themselves. With fifteen of us, I had to borrow some of Clara's utensils and plates, so the table is a bit of a hodgepodge. But no one cares. We've come together to celebrate as one big, blended family, not impress Martha Stewart.

After we've eaten enough to keep us full for hours to come, the kids disappear down the hall, and Clara clinks a spoon against her glass, rising to her feet. "I wanted to say a few words, if that's okay with you all?"

"Of course, honey. Go ahead," Mom says, and she throws me a smile that tells me how much she likes Clara.

"Thanks, Judy. First, thank you to Cade for hosting us all here today. It's been incredible to bring both your family"—she gestures at my mom, my sister, and her husband—"and my family together. I think we make a beautifully overcomplicated family tree. Families are both blood and chosen, and today, I think we've got the perfect mix of both, don't you?"

People laugh and several people voice their agreement.

"This has been quite a year for all of us. For me, being a chronic illness warrior has meant embracing all of life's possibilities, not just surviving them. Part of embracing those possibilities brought me to my job in social media at the Ice Breakers, and brought me to this guy." She grins at me.

I raise my hand. "That's me, in case you were wondering," I say, and win a laugh.

"I know I've only just met you today, and it's been wonderful to get to spend this time with you," she says to my family. "I want you to know that Cade has been the second chance I wasn't even looking for, coming into my life like a ray of flirty sunshine, never taking no for an answer, and showing me what a real man is. He might be a tough guy out there on the ice. He might be built like a small giant with more muscles than a Mr. Universe contestant. But this guy gets it. He gets *me*. And this Thanksgiving I am so very grateful for him." She swallows and her eyes sparkle with unshed tears, tears of joy and of love, tears that make me love her all the more.

Not that I thought that was possible.

She raises her glass. "So, before I get totally soppy—"

"Too late, sis," Keira says.

"Give me a break. I'm newly in love," Clara replies, and I reach out and take her hand in mine, giving it a squeeze. Clara smiles down at me with love in her eyes, and I feel it, right in my heart.

"Here's to you, all of you. Some of you have come from the other side of the country, some from just up the road. But it's wonderful to have you all here and I am so grateful for each and every one of you. To family."

"To family," everyone around the table echoes, holding their glasses aloft, and as we all take a sip and Clara sits back down, I sling my arm around the back of her chair and plant a kiss against her soft cheek.

"Nicely said, Triple," I say.

"Thanks, honey."

I take her free hand in mine, and together we sit, united as one.

Before I arrived in this small town, I had been living a deliberately shallow existence, keeping relationships short and meaningless, terrified of repeating my dad's destructive pattern. My womanizer-slash-party-boy lifestyle was my armor, allowing me to offer low expectations to any woman I became involved with, knowing that then I could never disappoint.

Meeting Clara, getting to know her and Benny and Hannah, showed me what real family looks like. Instead of the broken promises I grew up with from my dad, I've discovered the beauty of showing up consistently, of being there for the ones I love.

And I intend to keep on showing up, to keep on loving. Because here I've found my purpose, my heart. Moving to Maple Falls has given me the world. I'm part of something bigger than me and my hockey career. I'm part of something more meaningful and lasting. And I know, deep in my heart, this is precisely where I'm meant to be.

I've not just found love here in Maple Falls, population ten thousand.

I've found my home.

. . .

Do you want to know what happens next? For a BONUS EPILOGUE set in Cade and Clara's future, follow this link: https://dl.bookfunnel.com/l0ik81dwq5

NEXT BOOK IN THE LOVE IN MAPLE FALLS SERIES

GRAB the next book in the series where Cade's teammate and friend, Asher and Mabel get their chance at love in Anne Kemp's *Checking Mr. Wrong*.

She's a grump with a grudge. He's a sweetheart with a slapshot. Sparks were expected, but the fireworks? Pure magic.

. . .

Mabel

Returning to Maple Falls wasn't part of my five-year plan—or my backup plan. Or any plan, really. But here I am, back in my quirky hometown, dodging my mother's judgment and trying not to cringe every time someone mentions the viral moment. (Yes, that one. No, I don't want to talk about it.)

When my editor sends me to cover the NHL's shiny new team, the Ice Breakers, I'm all in—until I meet Asher Tremblay. He's their too-charming defenseman with a knack for wrecking my focus and my sanity. Equal parts infuriating and irresistible, but falling for him? Not on my agenda. Nope.

Asher

I've worked my whole life to make it in the NHL. A new team means a fresh start, and I won't let anything distract me—least of all a snarky reporter who seems determined to hate me on sight.

But the more I see Mabel, the more I want to know what's behind her walls. She's fire and chaos, and I've spent my whole life playing it safe. Maybe she's exactly what I need. I came to Maple Falls to chase my dream, but now all I want is her.

ALSO IN THE LOVE IN MAPLE FALLS SERIES

CAST OF CHARACTERS IN THE LOVE IN MAPLE FALLS SERIES

ASHER TREMBLAY: love interest is Mabel McCluskey; Position: Defense, #5. From Canada, played for the River City Renegades before being called up to the Ice Breakers.

Ashlyn Thompkins: love interest is Jamie Hayes; Grew up in Maple Falls across the street from Mabel McCluskey and next door to Clara and Keira Johnson; Mayor's daughter.

Bailey Porter: love interest is Carson Crane; a Maple Falls local and friends with Mabel, Neesha, and Clara Johnson. Works for the NHL. Maple butter maker.

Cade Lennox: love interest is Clara Johnson; Position: Right wingman, #44; played on the New York City Blades with Jamie Hayes.

. . .

Carson Crane: love interest is Bailey Porter; Position: Left wingman, #49. From Alabama, played for the Nebraska Knights, and was a last-minute transfer.

Clara Johnson: love interest is Cade Lennox; sister of Keira Johnson; grew up in Maple Falls across the street from Mabel McCluskey and next door to Ashlyn Thompkins; friends with Bailey Porter; CFS sufferer: Ice Breakers social media manager.

Clément Rivière: love interest is Marcy Fontaine. Position: Goalie, #95. Recently moved to the U.S.A. from France, where he played for the Paris Lions, to follow his American Dream.

Fiona Hale: love interest is Weston Smith. From New York City, visiting her aunt Denise Hale in Maple Falls. Knows Mabel through work connections in NYC.

Jamie Hayes: love interest is Ashlyn Thompkins; Position: Center, #33; played on the New York City Blades with Cade Lennox.

Lucian Lowe: love interest is Neesha Gilmore; Position: Defenseman, #7. Played on the Carolina Crushers with Dawson Hayes (series 1).

Mabel McCluskey: love interest is Asher Tremblay; daughter of town gossip Mary-Ellen McCluskey, high school friends with Neesha and Bailey. Knows Fiona through work connections in

NYC; grew up in Maple Falls across the street from Clara and Keira Johnson.

Marcy Fontaine: love interest is Clément Rivière; works at Happy Horizons ranch in exchange for room and board. Is the accountant for Town Hall and most of the folks in Maple Falls.

Neesha Gilmore: love interest is Lucian Lowe; a cupcake baker who lives in Maple Falls; works at the Falling for Books Cafe with Emmy Roberts (series 1).

Weston Smith: love interest is Fiona Hale; Position: Defense, #22. Former player with the Tennessee Wolves; knows Cooper Montgomery.

KATE'S HOCKEY ROMANCES

Kate O'Keeffe has written several hockey romances, all closed door, fun, and swoony, and all interconnected stories.

A second-chance romance between a hockey star and his high school sweetheart, set in a small town where sparks fly faster than slapshots

A forbidden love story between the team's social media manager and the hockey player she's not supposed to fall for—especially when her career and heart are both on the line. **On preorder, releasing August 20th**

A fake-feud holiday romcom about a single mom and a charming hockey player who agree to play enemies for the cameras—until real feelings crash the party

ALSO BY KATE O'KEEFFE

ROYAL ROMCOMS:

The Backup Princess

Royally Matched

The Royal Runaway

Royally Off-Limits

HOCKEY ROMCOMS:

Mistletoe Face Off

The Rebound Play

Offside and Off-Limits

SMALL TOWN ROMCOMS:

Faking It With the Grump

Faking It With My Best Friend

Faking It With the Guy Next Door

ROMCOMS SET IN BRITAIN:

Dating Mr. Darcy

Marrying Mr. Darcy

Falling for Another Darcy

Falling for Mr. Bingley (spin-off novella)

Never Fall for Your Back-Up Guy

Never Fall for Your Enemy

Never Fall for Your Fake Fiancé

Never Fall for Your One that Got Away

ROMCOMS SET IN NEW ZEALAND:

One Last First Date

Two Last First Dates

Three Last First Dates

Four Last First Dates

No More Bad Dates

No More Terrible Dates

No More Horrible Dates

CO-AUTHORED WITH MELISSA BALDWIN:

One Way Ticket

WRITING AS LACEY SINCLAIR:

Manhattan Cinderella

The Right Guy

ABOUT THE AUTHOR

Kate O'Keeffe is a *USA Today* bestselling author known for her fun, feel-good romantic comedies brimming with humor, heart, and happily ever afters. A native of New Zealand, Kate has crafted numerous popular series, garnering a devoted international readership.

With a flair for witty banter and irresistible heroines navigating the ups and downs of modern dating, Kate's novels showcase strong friendships, comedic entanglements, and of course the sometimes bumpy but always hopeful road to love.

When she's not writing, Kate can often be found reading romcoms, binging her favourite shows, or spending time with her friends and family in the beautiful Hawke's Bay region of New Zealand.